"Did I frighten you?"
the large man asked gently,
stepping into the room.

When the stranger walked out of the shadows, he didn't look nearly so dark and menacing, though he was big and muscular. His thick brown hair was cut short but still hinted of curl, and his eyes were green. He didn't appear to be a thief or a murderer. In fact, he acted as if he was supposed to be in this house, right where he was. His confidence unnerved Lily.

His gaze was markedly friendly as he knelt beside her daughter. Lily's stomach turned over like a tidal wave, her protective instinct surging and waning in nauseating rhythm.

"Mr. MacCormack, this was not at all the entrance I had anticipated," Lily's mother snapped abrasively, clearly vexed. "I thought we had agreed you would begin your service tomorrow morning."

Lily's gaze shot to her mother. "You know this man?"

Books by Deb Kastner

Love Inspired

A Holiday Prayer #46
Daddy's Home #55
Black Hills Bride #90
The Forgiving Heart #113
A Daddy At Heart #140
A Perfect Match #164
The Christmas Groom #195
Hart's Harbor #210
Undercover Blessings #284

DEB KASTNER

is the wife of a Reformed Episcopal minister, so it was natural for her to find her niche in the Christian romance market. She enjoys tackling the issues of faith and trust within the context of a romance. Her characters range from upbeat and humorous to (her favorite) dark and brooding heroes. Her plots range widely from a playful romp to a deeply emotional story.

When she's not writing, she enjoys spending time with her husband and three girls and, whenever she can manage, attending regional dinner theater and Broadway musicals on tour.

UNDERCOVER BLESSINGS

DEB KASTNER

Steeple
Hill®

Published by Steeple Hill Books™

STEEPLE HILL BOOKS

Steeple
Hill®

ISBN 0-373-87294-1

UNDERCOVER BLESSINGS

www.SteepleHill.com

Printed in U.S.A.

The Lord is my light and my salvation;
Whom shall I fear?
The Lord is the strength of my life;
Of whom shall I be afraid?

—*Psalms* 27:1

To the phenomenal, multitalented Broadway legend
TERRENCE MANN, whose rich-voiced,
intensely powerful music weaves warmly
through every word of this book.
Thanks for giving me the inspiration to be my best.

Chapter One

"**Y**ou *know* why I didn't want to do this!" Lily Montague Larson, now going by her maiden name once again, leveled her mother with a seething glare that she did not acknowledge with so much as a word or a wave. Adora was stoic, definitely not the type of mother who baked cookies and welcomed family into her house.

"And you," the aged and ever-so-correct Adora Montague countered in a tone that not only ignored her daughter's sharp emotional state, but subtly indicated that she, the elder and ultimately wiser woman, had won the argument even as she was speaking, "know exactly why it *must* be done this way."

Lily hated it when her mother took that tone with her, effortlessly shaving off the years of armor she'd carefully built around herself and making her feel once again like a little girl, a girl without the self-esteem to stand up to Adora.

And she hated it even more when she knew her mother was right.

It had been ten years since, at age eighteen and ripe for adventure, Lily had walked out of her mother's house, shunning the fancy living, maids and butlers, and the money Adora held over her head in her trust fund, dangling it like bait to a hamster spinning hopelessly on a wheel.

She had not looked back.

Not even when things got rough. Not even when her husband died and left her with a baby to raise all by herself.

Now she was home and looking for help…from her mother of all people.

And it grated on her. More than she'd imagined it would, if that were possible. Every muscle in her body was quivering, screaming at her to run out of the house.

"If it wasn't for Abigail—" Lily began, but Adora cut her off.

"But it *is* about Abigail." She motioned to the sweet, curly-headed blond seven-year-old girl sound asleep on a plush white sofa in the adjoining room. Adora gazed sternly at Lily. "Right now, everything is about that little girl."

Lily gritted her teeth so hard her jaw ached. Wasn't it just like her mother to state the obvious.

"Don't you think I know that?" she rasped, turning away from her mother's know-it-all gaze.

"Of course you know," Adora said. "Your first thought is for Abigail, as well."

It wasn't a concession—Lily knew that much for certain.

Adora Montague never *conceded* to anything. And it wasn't kindness, or even love for her granddaughter, that made the older woman so eager to accept Lily and Abigail into her home as semi-permanent guests.

It was *control*.

Lily wanted, for at least the hundredth time in the last two hours, ever since Jonah, the footman/butler, had brought in their luggage and Lily had tucked her small, sleeping daughter onto the divan, to say it was a mistake, that they shouldn't be here, that they were leaving as soon as Abigail could handle more travel.

But she knew she wouldn't.

The poor child had experienced so little sleep lately that the long road trip from Maryland to Georgia had, in a way, been a blessed relief for both of them. Abigail slept well in the car, and they were going away from Washington, D.C., where she'd been in a mysterious, tragic accident.

Lily hoped her daughter had found at least some small measure of peace.

"How is Abigail doing with all this?" Adora asked,

as if following Lily's thoughts. "How has she been feeling these days?"

"She's not," Lily snapped, wrapping her arms around herself. And it was true. Abigail was keeping her feelings tucked deep inside, not even able consciously to acknowledge them.

Lily likewise kept her thoughts completely to herself.

"I was referring to her medical progress," her mother said in a voice as dry and parched as the scorching heat of the desert in full daylight. "What have the doctors said about her progress?"

"Her *emotional* state and her medical progress are one in the same, or so the FBI child psychologists are telling me," Lily said. "Whatever is causing her to block out the traumatic experience she had on the playground in Washington, D.C., is also what is keeping her from being able to walk."

Adora huffed and shook her head. "Sounds like hogwash to me."

Lily laughed dryly. "Yeah, it does to me, too."

Amazing.

She and her mother had finally agreed on something. And Adora always knew the perfect turn of phrase to put her thoughts into words. Unlike Lily, who had learned her best course of action was to keep her mouth shut.

Lily smothered a smile, knowing her mother would ask about it.

"But I do agree with the FBI on one point," Adora said firmly, her gaze locking with Lily's.

This was one topic Lily didn't really want to discuss.

"What's that?" Lily asked, her shoulders tensing.

"Abigail needs protection. *Real* protection from a *real* enemy. Especially if—once she begins to remember what happened."

"I'm here, aren't I?" Lily snapped. "I'll protect her with my own life if I have to. And now she's got you by her side, as well."

"Right," Adora agreed dryly, tapping her cane on the hardwood floor for emphasis. "In case you haven't noticed, Lil, I'm nothing more threatening than a harmless old lady."

Lily snorted. That was the first truly funny thing she'd heard in weeks. "I hate to be the one to break it to you, Mama, but with your money and influence in the community, you're quietly known around here as the Dragon Lady."

She immediately felt a stroke of remorse at repeating such an unkind remark, and was formulating an apology when to her surprise, Adora chuckled.

"I worked hard for that moniker, young lady, and it serves a good purpose. Hopefully, it will provide us with some privacy now."

She paused and stroked her chin, and Lily could swear a spark came into those old blue-gray eyes. "But I still maintain, whatever *you* say about it, that we're just a couple of unprotected women. A little extra muscle couldn't hurt."

Oh, yes it could, Lily thought, but she left her opinion unspoken. Her scars were her own, and her mother would never understand.

"I only want to do what's right for my granddaughter. I'm thinking of Abigail first and foremost in everything, you know."

"I know, Mama."

As much as Lily hated to admit it, what her mother said was true. Adora had her odd ways, but she did put Abigail first in everything. It was clear she cared about her granddaughter, even if she showed it only in her own eccentric way.

Lily would just have to make sure her mother's controlling personality didn't reach into Abigail's personal world. She would protect her daughter from such influences.

Lily was an adult now and knew better. She didn't have to take Adora's word as law, and neither did Abigail. If she had to, she would fight back.

Suddenly, a high, terrified shriek emitted from the next room, instantly bringing both Lily and Adora to their feet, staring at each other in shock.

Blood roared in Lily's ears, and adrenaline had her shaking. Then her heart stopped beating completely for a good long moment and her breath left her body in a rush as the piercing screams continued to emanate from the adjoining room.

Abigail.

Lily whirled and dashed for her daughter, the sharp sound of Adora's cane pounding against the bare wooden floor clicking at her heels in cadence with her pulse.

The sound was oddly and unusually loud to Lily, even over the pounding of her heart. And even over the cry of her sweet little girl. She focused on the stark tip of the cane as it hit wood, trying to coax her mind into rational thinking.

As she scrambled toward her daughter, she continued to try to persuade her mind to focus, to make mental notes of the situation as she entered the room, something useful and not frantically ineffective.

Something to help her help her daughter out of whatever horrible situation was present. Her mind could conjure up many such circumstances.

There were no big-lug Secret Service men posted in the corners wearing sunglasses even in the dull lamplight of the room. No muscle-bound FBI guys with transmitters strapped to their belts and mini-Glocks poised to save the day.

As Lily had so aptly pointed out to her mother, *she* was all Abigail had for protection. There wasn't even a gun in the house, and up until this moment, Lily had been glad for that fact. Now she sent up a frantic prayer to God that *she* would be enough.

The room was glowing from the light of one lamp lit low, and it appeared to be empty except for Abigail, who was lying spine-ridged stiff on the sofa, her screams having ebbed to quiet sobs as she covered her head with her arms.

Lily's hair was still on end, not just on the back of her neck, but on her arms and scalp as well. Abigail's scream had sounded *real,* much more than just the result of a bad dream or from being suddenly startled awake and not knowing where she was.

Even now, she was obviously traumatized about something. She might be paralyzed from the waist down, but her arms were shaking and, when Lily brought her hands from her head, her eyes were as wide and frightened as large blue bowling balls.

Lily's gut feeling was that this situation was something else entirely.

Something to do with Abigail's trauma. Something dangerous.

She pushed her feelings to the back of her mind, knowing her smart, sensitive daughter would be able to read any sign of distress on her face.

Lily needed to stay in control, now. Her daughter was looking to her for strength. And she would find it, no matter how scared Lily felt for her daughter.

"What happened?" she asked gently as she straightened the covers around Abigail's shoulders and wrapped the limp, fragile child in her arms.

"There's a man in the house, Mommy," Abigail answered with a shudder.

Lily's eyes widened despite her best efforts, and her pulse roared. "A man?" she repeated, hoping against hope she'd heard it wrong.

"I saw him. Over there. He stopped and looked at me." She pointed to the open double doors that led to a hallway across from the room Lily and Adora had been occupying.

"Are you sure it wasn't Jonah, sweetheart?" Adora asked. "You know how silly that butler can be. He's always floating around here and there like a ghost, not making a single sound. Why, he's given me a fright or two myself a few times."

Abigail shook her head vehemently, her eyes sparkling with righteous indignation that her voice wasn't being heard. "It wasn't Jonah. I know it wasn't Jonah. Mom, you believe me, don't you?"

"How can you be so certain?" Lily asked gently, feeling a tug of pride for her brave, strong daughter. "You were awakened from a deep sleep, after all. Perhaps you saw something else and thought it was a man. Maybe it was nothing at all. Could it have been part of your dream?"

Abigail pinned Lily with a look that let her know just how ludicrous her little girl thought she was. "The man I saw in the doorway was real, Mom. He was a lot bigger than Jonah," she said firmly, meeting both her mother's and grandmother's eyes before they could find the words to argue the point further.

"But—" Lily said and was cut off.

"I wasn't dreaming," Abigail continued, pausing dramatically and looking at each of them as she crossed her arms over her chest, "Because the man I saw before is standing in the doorway right now."

"Did I frighten you?" the large man asked in a gentle bass voice, stepping into the room from the darkness of the hallway.

He had loomed like a monster when Lily first saw him but when the stranger walked out of the shadows, he didn't look nearly so dark and menacing, though he was big and muscular.

His thick dark-brown hair was cut short and combed in a military style, but it still hinted of curl. His eyes were large and green, not the beady-eyed black Lily had imagined in that one outstretched moment of her darkest nightmare.

He didn't appear to be a thief or a murderer. In fact, he acted as if he was supposed to be in this house, right where he was. He looked chagrined, but comfortable and his confidence unnerved her.

His gaze was markedly friendly as he knelt beside Abigail. Lily's stomach turned over like a tidal wave, her protective instinct surging and waning in nauseating rhythm. Part of her wanted to tackle the man, though such an action would do little good.

Still, she held her breath as the man approached her daughter.

"Mr. MacCormack, this was not at all the entrance I had anticipated," Adora snapped abrasively, clearly vexed, but obviously not at all surprised at the man's appearance. "I thought we had agreed you would begin your service tomorrow morning."

Lily's gaze shot to her mother's. "You *know* this man?"

"Well, of course I know him," Adora said, waving her daughter off as if she had asked the silliest of questions. "You don't imagine for one moment I would allow a complete stranger to enter my house."

Lily wanted to scream in frustration at a mother who was more put out that Lily thought she couldn't run her household than she was that a strange man had nearly frightened them all to death.

She moved to her daughter's side and gently propped Abigail to a sitting position with pillows behind her back for support. Smiling softly, she planted a kiss on her delicate forehead.

She made a point of not looking at the man kneeling by the sofa, though she could feel his eyes upon her, unnerving her.

"Are you a ghost?" Abigail asked the big man, her eyes narrowing in rapt consideration.

The man's bright-green eyes filled with amusement at her question, while at the same time he kept his expression perfectly serious. He had clearly been around children before and was being careful not to look as if he was mocking her.

"No, Miss Abby, I'm not a ghost." He slowly held out his hand to her, insisting she touch him so she could feel he was real. "See? I am every bit as real and human as you are."

The little girl nodded and, looking thoughtful, reached out a finger and poked him cautiously in the chest. "But you know my name," she pointed out with the innocent wisdom of a child.

He nodded. "That's true."

"Then you must be an angel," she concluded with a happy smile. "Are you my guardian angel, Mr...? Mr...? Mack—"

"You can call me Kevin," he said, beaming back at the child, and then flashing Lily a happy grin that made her stomach flip over.

"If you want me to be your guardian angel, Miss Abby," Kevin continued, his voice serious and courteous, "then I guess that's just what I am."

In Lily's childhood she'd often pictured angel guardians standing in the corners of her bedroom keeping watch over her at night. In her young fantasies, her angels all had strong names, like Gabriel and Michael.

The man before her had the height and the muscular build to rival anything she'd imagined the heavenly hosts might bear.

But *Kevin?*

Lily shook her head and smothered a smile, not yet ready to indicate her approval.

"I've got a problem, though, Abby," Kevin said with a lazy smile that deepened the lines on his five-o'clock shadow and revealed a dimple in his right cheek. Not to mention the laugh lines on his eyes.

"What is your problem?" the child asked brightly, as full of concern for him as if she had no problems of her own to deal with. She had obviously already completely taken to the man.

Kevin stood and turned his back to the little girl, then did a small series of dance-like steps to indicate he was attempting to jump off the ground. He even started flapping his arms like a bird, when nothing else apparently worked.

Abigail was in stitches.

The man grinned. "You see? My wings are so tiny you can't even see them."

"That's okay," Abigail said sympathetically.

"It is?"

"Sure. Haven't you watched the movies, Mr. Kevin? Angels have to *earn* their wings."

Kevin snapped his fingers. "So that's what it is. I was wondering what was up with these annoying absent wings of mine."

"Of course, silly. Didn't you know? It's in all the movies."

"So it is." Kevin cocked a hand to his chin as if considering Abigail's words. "Well," he said slowly, "I now know everything, thanks to you. But I'm going to need a lot of help, don't you think?"

Lily smothered a laugh on the back of her hand. If the man was aiming for angelhood, it looked to her as though he had a long way to go. *Help* was the understatement of the century.

"Oh, we'll help you, won't we, Mommy?" Abigail hadn't sounded so excited since she'd had her accident, and it was wonderful to hear.

All eyes immediately swung to Lily, even Adora's, who had one eyebrow cocked in mild amusement. Kevin was just giving her a straight, smooth grin, his eyes petitioning her to play along.

Lily cringed inwardly at the position she'd inadvertently been placed into. While she couldn't exactly dislike the man, she certainly didn't trust him. As far as she was concerned, he was going to have to look elsewhere for help earning his wings.

For all she knew he had horns growing under that thick dark-brown hair of his, and she wasn't about to take any chances.

There *was* the fact that her mother had apparently arranged for this man to behave. Adora never did anything halfway, so Lily knew this *Kevin* must have had, at the very least, a thorough background check before he'd entered the grounds, never mind the house. Who knew the lengths to which her mother would go in such a situation to keep her granddaughter safe.

Adora was, in fact, looking quite smug at the moment as she watched the interaction between Abigail and Kevin.

"May I speak to you for a moment Mr.—uh—Kevin?" Lily asked, stammering to avoid the last name she had quickly forgotten in all the excitement.

She needed to know what was going on, and her mother was obviously not in a hurry to enlighten her.

He smiled accommodatingly. "Absolutely, ma'am. Just give me another moment or two with my patient before we go, will you?"

His *patient?*

Lily was stunned.

"I've got a present for you," he told Abigail. He smiled secretively and jammed his hand in the front pocket of his blue jeans.

Lily acknowledged belatedly his pale-blue scrub shirt, something she realized she should have noticed much earlier. Had she been so lost in admiring the breadth of his shoulders that she'd forgotten to pay attention to the *important* details?

She shot a questioning glance at her mother, but Adora only smiled back in that regal way she had, tipped her chin in the air and purposefully returned her attention to Kevin and Abigail.

"I'm going to be hanging around here every day from now on," Kevin informed Abigail, his deep voice firm and friendly. He was sincerely trying, and as Lily gauged it with some good measure of success, to reassure her little girl of her safety.

He scored points there, but she still didn't trust him.

"And obviously," he continued, confirming Lily's thoughts, "as your self-proclaimed angel, part of my job will be to protect you."

Abigail nodded, her big blue eyes even wider than usual.

"But sometimes, especially at night, you can't help but feel afraid when you're alone. We all feel that way from time to time." His gentle statement made Lily's heart sink, and wiped the smile from Abigail's face. "That's why I got you this."

Kevin pulled his fist from his pocket and dropped something into Abigail's hand, holding his palm over hers, molding it there.

Finally, he backed away, his gaze not leaving Abigail's face as she stared at her palm and smiled a secret smile that only included him. For a moment, the world was theirs.

Kevin's gaze met Lily's for one moment before he turned to Adora. "If there isn't anything else, ma'am, I'd like to excuse myself. I have a lot to do in preparation for my new position as Abby's nurse."

"Like what?" Lily asked before she could think better of it.

She was and always had been insatiably curious about everything around her, and this situation was certainly still an enigma to her in a number of ways.

Who was this man, really?

Kevin stalled for a moment, his eyes wide, and Lily knew instinctively she'd somehow caught him off guard. The only question was, *why?*

Now she was doubly interested in his answer to her off-the-cuff question. What was Kevin MacCormack hiding behind his gleaming green eyes?

To what capacity was Kevin working for Adora? And why hadn't Lily been informed of this situation earlier? She wasn't happy to be left out of the loop.

More likely he was in cahoots with her mother, Lily suspected. But other than being a great deal too large and too masculine for Lily's idea of a nurse, she had to admit he was pretty good.

Not that she'd actually seen him do anything resembling nursing, but he *had* won over her daughter with a single charming smile. And she could tell he was serious about his job by the sweet, delicate way he handled the little girl, and by the respectful way he interacted with her.

"Mr. MacCormack?" she reminded him tersely. She might have been deep in thought, but Kevin still looked stunned and speechless. She had merely asked him a simple question about his job.

He shrugged. "Well, you know…"

He was stalling again.

"Actually," Lily said, "I don't know. Tell me, what does a nurse have to do to get ready to go in the morning?"

"Uh—get my stethoscope, blood-pressure cuff, bandages. That sort of thing."

"I'm certain my mother has told you that we have all the latest in medical supplies already on hand."

"Oh, yeah. Yeah," he said with more conviction. "Of course. But I have a few pieces of equipment of my own I like to use. I just want to make sure everything is in order for my first official day of work. I'm very thorough, you know."

Lily didn't miss the sideswiping look Kevin gave to her mother, nor Adora's quick, clamped-down response to the petition for help in his gaze.

"Let the poor man go, Lily. Just because you obsess over everything doesn't mean the rest of the world has to act that way."

"Oh, no, ma'am, it's fine," Kevin assured Adora. "She has every right to ask me questions. She's only trying to protect her daughter. I wouldn't expect anything less from her."

Adora huffed and whirled on her heels, then glided from the room without another word, the only sound the click of her cane.

Kevin, his eyebrows raised, turned to look at Lily.

She shrugged. It was as close to an apology as he was going to get.

He grinned, his gaze full of amusement. His eyes were the oddest, most beautiful color, she thought as she stared at him. They were a deep green, the color of evergreen in winter. And they were striking in contrast to his thick dark brown hair.

He smiled again and tipped an imaginary hat at her, then let himself out the front door, whistling under his breath.

There wasn't going to be a personal meeting between the two of them tonight. But she would be sure she had the opportunity to speak to Kevin in private and give him her impression of this situation.

Soon.

Lily switched mental gears as she turned to Abigail. The little girl was still smiling and cupping her present from Kevin in her palm.

"What did he give you, sweetheart?" Lily asked, suddenly curious. She moved to her daughter's side and gingerly perched on the end of the sofa, peering at her daughter's palm.

What had Kevin given her that was so special, so mysterious that her daughter was hesitant to share the secret with her own mother?

"He gave me this," Abigail said, and opened her fingers slowly.

Lily gasped.

On her little girl's palm lay a gold pendant in the shape of a guardian angel.

Chapter Two

"I wouldn't be honest if I didn't say I'm not completely comfortable with this situation," Kevin "Mack" MacCormack said to a thoughtfully silent Adora Montague, who had not uttered so much as a single word since she had met him at the back door at midnight. "I understand why we have to keep Lily in the dark about this, but it just doesn't feel right."

He'd politely made his exit after meeting Lily and Abigail for the first time. He might not have angel's wings, but he'd flown out of that house like a man on fire, his feet barely touching the ground.

There was a lot that Adora Montague had left out of her simple scenario when she'd presented it to him the day he'd first agreed to take on the case. She had sounded so thorough, but there was no way to explain the dynamics he had encountered this evening.

He'd been on the job ten years and thought he'd seen everything, but he hadn't been ready to walk into the Montague mansion and find Lily Montague staring back at him with her big brown eyes. So striking.

So stoic.

So *angry*.

He'd been thinking only of the child, of her needs—and that had been his mistake. But even if he'd prepared himself for Abigail's mother, he doubted he would ever have been ready for meeting Lily. She was beyond comprehension.

It wasn't that he'd never seen the raw, unhitched emotions she wore over her like a thick cloak. He'd been assigned similar cases in the past, at least in theory. He had seen the worn and ravaged faces of mothers and fathers emotionally ransacked by terrible acts of hate and evil beyond their control that had affected their children.

And he'd hardened his heart to it long ago.

A man couldn't do work like this for a living and get personally involved. The ravages of emotion would tear him apart in the end, and he knew better than to lower the shield, even just a little. He had to protect himself, and cool, calculated distance was the way he had chosen to keep his heart intact.

So why then did looking into Lily Montague's eyes make him want to fold her into his arms and hold her as tightly as he could, to reassure her that hope and help were near.

A desire within him wanted to whisper in her ear, to assure her nothing would ever harm her or her precious Abby again—as if he could make those promises in good faith.

His throat tightened with emotion, but suddenly he cut loose and chuckled.

Trying to comfort a woman like Lily would be like trying to embrace an angry porcupine. Heaven's thunder, the woman would kick him in the shins and punch him in the nose before he could whisper a single solitary word of nonsense into her ear.

Lily didn't want his help, nor the small comfort he could offer with his protection. She'd already made that fact abundantly clear.

Besides, he was a professional.

And he was working undercover.

Lily did not know about his real job, and for her own sake as well as the sake of little Abby, he had to make certain she could not discover who he really was and why he was here.

To her, he must always remain the gentle nurse. At least that was the truth, he had gotten his nurse training and degree in the army.

"Were you planning on coming back from that faraway planet you're on, or should I just leave you standing here gawking for the rest of the night?"

The dry voice of Adora broke harshly into his thoughts.

"I beg your pardon, ma'am," he said, unconsciously rubbing a hand against his ribs where his sidearm was kept. "I was just thinking."

"I thought perhaps my esteemed company had put you to sleep."

Heat flared to his face at her blunt reminder, but when he met her gaze, he saw a glimmer of amusement in the gray depths of her eyes. Despite himself, he smiled at her. There was more to the elderly Montague than met the eye. He would have to remind himself of that on a regular basis.

He attempted to switch gears, change the subject to something besides himself.

"Your daughter is quite a woman." He thought it just as well to be up-front about everything, including what he thought about Lily.

"Yes." Adora nodded slowly. "I suppose I should have warned you."

"You gave me the facts."

The old lady snorted her disdain for his illusory state-ment. "Facts don't paint the whole picture. You FBI guys ought to know that better than anyone."

He chuckled. "Point well taken."

"So you want to go running with your tail tucked after just one night." It was a statement, not a question, and Mack's gall rose.

He crossed his arms over his chest and glowered down at her. Every nerve ending in his body was sparking with indignation. "I've never run from a challenge in my life, and I don't intend to start now."

She chuckled, a dry, crackling sound from the back of her throat. "Glad to hear it."

Mack scratched his cheek, considering his words carefully. "I'll stay, but I've got to tell you I feel wrong about misrepresenting myself and my intentions to your daughter."

"You mean you feel bad for lying."

Don't hesitate to call a spade a spade, Mack thought, inwardly heaving a sigh.

"Call it what you want. It doesn't seem right to me. One of the questions you asked me before I came on was about my faith. I told you then, and I'm telling you now—I'm a Christian man, born and raised in the church. And I'm wrestling with this issue, with deceiving Lily."

"I can see that, young man," Adora said, her voice contemplative and low. "But if you really think about it, isn't *all* the undercover work you do for the FBI lying, in a sense?"

The question hit Mack with the impact of a bullet straight to the heart—without the expediency of a bulletproof vest.

He'd been so busy playing cops and robbers, being the man in the white hat who sacked the bad guy and made the world a better place, that until this moment, he'd never seriously considered the moral implications of working undercover.

It was just something he did because he was ordered to do so by his superiors. It was the only way to gain control of some ugly situations.

It was the lesser of two evils.

Or was it?

"You are going to save my granddaughter, Mr. Mac-Cormack," Adora said in the slow, rich, even tenor she always used. "It is your duty, and now you can see other reasons this case is so important."

She paused and looked him in the eye. "You are going to find the people who did this terrible thing to Abigail, and you are going to bring them to justice."

She coughed twice and then remained silent. For just one moment, as Adora stood with a wrinkled hand to her chest, Mack thought he could glimpse the true agony of her heart.

She didn't speak it. It was something a woman like Adora Montague would never do. She was being strong for her daughter and granddaughter.

But the pain was there, deep and hidden away.

"Here's your room," Adora indicated with an elegant swish of her arm. "Just as you requested. I hope you'll find everything you need to make yourself at *home.*"

Mack didn't miss the emphasis. What he had requested in his room could hardly be called comfortable, much less home, and they both knew it. He wasn't here on vacation, and his living quarters proved it.

Adora raised one eyebrow and studied him intensely.

"What?" he asked when she continued to stare at him without speaking. She was making him more nervous by not talking than if she said what she felt.

She put a finger to her chin and tapped slowly, half the rhythm of his rapid heartbeat. "If we are very blessed, young man, and God shines His light down on us," she said, "you will save my daughter Lily, as well."

Adora turned, leaning heavily on her cane, yet still managing to look graceful and dignified for all her age and ailments.

Mack stood watching her limp rhythmically away, her last statement still tumbling like a windstorm through his mind.

Slowly, he became aware of his surroundings, the room he would be calling home for the next few days or weeks. He hadn't expected a posh, grand room with a king-sized bed and a soft comforter.

Which was a good thing, because what he could see in the darkened room was a small cot and a wool blanket. He'd probably have to dangle his legs off the end of the ancient thing.

His first thought was to turn on a light, but he stood quietly in the dark instead, his arms crossed tightly over his chest. He stared tight-lipped at his stark cot as his eyes adjusted to the darkness, intimately aware of the thousands of dollars of technological equipment lining the walls. Finally, he moved to stare silently into the full-length, two-way mirror through which he could see Abby sleeping soundly in her bedroom.

From any angle in the small room, she was visible, and thus protected.

With the single punch of a switch, he could be by the little girl's side to guard and protect her.

Here, in this small, secluded room Adora had had built for just this purpose, he could watch over the darling blond-haired child like the guardian angel she thought he was.

Yes, he could protect Abby.

But Lily?

He wasn't so sure about Lily.

What had Adora meant by her statement?

Jonah announced *Nurse* MacCormack just as the towering grandfather clock in the foyer struck 8:00 a.m.

Lily covered a yawn with the back of her hand. Well, the man was prompt, anyway. More good marks for him, she supposed.

She had never been a morning person, and even though she'd spent years going through the motions of putting her daughter on the school bus and getting herself to work dressed *and* on time, it had never become second nature to her. She was often still banding her watch to her wrist or pinning earrings to her ears as she dashed down the hallway on her way to the Senate floor to testify on some aspect of a bill.

She didn't usually feel awake until sometime in the afternoon, and she did her best thinking late at night when all was quiet.

But today, she wanted to be at her best—fully alert, completely dressed from shoes to makeup and mentally at full steam ahead. Even if it was only eight o'clock in the morning.

If this MacCormack character was going to invade her life—and more importantly, Abigail's life—she was going to be ready for him.

Of course, to be fair, Lily had to admit—at least to herself—that he'd done absolutely nothing to warrant her inherent distrust of him.

Abigail clearly adored him.

Adora consented to his presence.

He had been nothing but polite, kind and gentle. And to add to that, he was certainly the best-looking man Lily had seen in a long time, and she had seen a lot of handsome men working in Washington, D.C.

Kevin was definitely good-looking, but in a more rugged, outdoorsy kind of way.

Maybe that's why her hackles were up. She well knew her attraction—*fatal* attraction—to rugged men.

And where had that impulse got her?

Here.

Whatever it was that was summoning her inner dander, Lily had learned long ago to listen to her instincts. Too many bad things had happened to the people she had loved in her lifetime. She wasn't about to let anything else happen to her or the ones she loved.

Especially Abigail. No one must ever hurt her little girl again.

Lily tensed as Mr. MacCormack stepped from the foyer and into the living room, where she was waiting for him, half holding her breath, her fists clenched at her sides.

Adora had left instructions the night before for Mr. MacCormack, whom she considered an employee and not a guest. Consequently, she hadn't found it necessary to change her usual routine of enjoying a cup of hot cocoa and a fresh sweet roll delivered by a housemaid to the comfort of her bedroom.

"It's a brisk morning out there," MacCormack said by way of greeting, blowing on his fingers and rubbing his hands together for warmth. "That wind has got a good chill to it."

"Might I suggest a pair of gloves?" Lily asked dryly, trying to hold in her smile.

She couldn't. Her grin went ear to ear as she surveyed the man. His cheeks were red from the wind, and his green eyes bright with the cold. His dark-brown hair was tousled like a young boy's locks, and she fought the peculiar desire to smooth his hair back with the palm of her hand.

At Lily's words, Kevin gave a startled look to his bare, open hands. He looked back at her, meeting her gaze numbly for a moment, and then suddenly roared and slapped a hand against his thighs.

"You know, Miss Lily, I don't even own a pair of gloves. At least," he amended hastily, "not a pair of winter gloves."

"I see," she said, attempting to control her smile so she didn't look like a fool.

"I did, however, bring something warm and furry to help keep the cold out."

Lily cocked a brow. He grinned and gestured to the foyer. "I come bearing gifts."

She frowned and perched her hands on her hips. "I'm sorry. Did you say *gifts?*"

"For Abby. Wait right here." He disappeared into the foyer.

Lily wondered what she should do. Her mother would not appreciate whatever effort Kevin had gone to, and would no doubt not approve of any more gift-giving on Kevin's behalf. He was an employee, and there was a certain decorum that separated them.

Then again, Abigail had seen too little true generosity in her young life.

How could one little gift hurt? One little gift for her precious, ailing daughter who had seen so much pain in her young life.

That fantasy was quickly extinguished as Kevin re-entered the room laden with a huge black teddy bear half the size of the man holding it and a large bag of gift boxes which looked as if they contained a curly-haired blond doll and an assortment of clothing and baby-doll items.

Lily shook her head in amazement. What would the man do next?

Her mental question was quickly answered as he stepped forward and thrust the huge, fluffy black bear into her arms.

"You take this one, and I'll bring the doll and stuff. I don't think I can handle both presents at once. I can't see around the bear, and I know I'll crash into something expensive and irreplaceable. I can't do it all by myself, that's for sure."

"Of course you can't." Lily snickered. She couldn't see around the bear either. She shrugged and shook her head again in amusement. She couldn't stop chuckling at the man's crazy antics.

Kevin MacCormack's M.O. was above and beyond.

Part of her desperately wanted to throw the black teddy bear down on the nearest piece of furniture and give Kevin a big hug.

The other, no doubt more sensible part of her, wanted to take him firmly by the shoulders, turn him around, and push him right out the front door before he caused a moment's more havoc—and she had no doubt there would be plenty of it—in Abigail's life.

In *her* life.

Although, to be brutally honest, the havoc probably affected her more and Abigail less. Somehow she doubted her daughter's reaction to the giant teddy bear would be the undeniable racing of her heart that Lily herself was experiencing.

Lily decided what she was feeling had nothing to do with the man and all to do with stress. It had been a long few weeks, and the end was nowhere in sight. Surely that was an absolutely logical explanation for her erratic heart rhythms.

Who wouldn't be an emotional dishrag after what she'd been through? A pair of shoulders Kevin's size, especially when accompanied by the genuinely empathizing look he was now giving her, was almost more inducement to give into her fragile emotions than she could resist.

Kevin was definitely a temptation.

But, for better or for worse, Lily Montague leaned on no one. She had decided that long ago, and she wasn't changing her mind for a pair of wide, sympathetic green eyes.

She gave him a wavering smile and nodded toward the bedroom. "I'm sure our patient will be thrilled with your gifts."

She didn't mention her mother. She would deal with Adora later.

Lily didn't want Kevin to get into trouble with her mother. The man was a Good Samaritan, and he didn't deserve Adora's wrath.

They could see from the hallway that Abigail was

covered up to her chin by a thick, soft comforter, watching the slim plasma television wired up into one of the top corners of her room. She loved the shows about dogs. She could name every breed and list numerous facts about each one.

Lily thought she might have a future veterinarian on her hands, or perhaps even a dog trainer for movies in Hollywood.

But Abigail quickly lost interest in her program when Lily walked in carting the gigantic plush bear.

"Oh, Mommy. Is that for me?" she exclaimed, clapping her hands. She looked as if she wanted to jump out of bed with joy.

If only she could.

"Compliments of Nurse Kevin," Lily said, bringing the bear to rest beside her precocious daughter, who was beaming with a smile. "Pretty nice of him, don't you think?"

"He takes care of me," she said simply in a trusting voice. "That's his job."

"Don't you forget it," Kevin said in a bright, rich bass as he entered the room. "And that's not all, love. I brought you a doll and some frilly-nilly stuff to dress her up in."

The little girl squealed with delight.

"I can't promise you I did a good job picking out a good doll, though, Abby. It's my first time with dolls. I had no idea there were so many to choose from. I picked one with pretty blond curls, just like yours. I hope you like her."

"Oh," Abigail exclaimed, clapping both hands over her mouth. "Mr. Kevin, she's perfect."

Now, Lily noticed with a sudden odd swelling in her throat, it was *Mr.* Kevin doing the beaming. She had to chuckle at the picture of her precious little girl and this big sweetheart of a nurse.

She found it wasn't as difficult to accept Kevin in their lives as she'd first thought it would be.

Perhaps it was because of his gentle manner. He was kind and soft-spoken, and constantly thought of others before himself. He smiled all the time and laughed frequently.

He wasn't a threat to her.

Despite her earlier fears and despite his looks, he obviously wasn't the kind of man she would typically be attracted to—the rough, dangerous bad boy who thrived on living on the edge—an edge that could slice a woman's heart clean through.

That kind of man lived on adrenaline. He was a perpetual risk-taker. Those men were the firemen, the policemen, the FBI agents of the world.

She couldn't help it if she loved them. But she could do something about it and run the other direction at the mere sight of such a man.

Lily swallowed hard and forced herself from thoughts of Abigail's father, her late husband.

David had been dead for just over seven years now. She knew in her heart, for Abigail's sake if nothing else, it was long past time to move on with her life, begin new relationships and experience new emotions.

But no matter how she tried to break away from the memories of her time with David, the good times and the romantic times they'd shared, she couldn't seem to lose the anger.

And that anger, that horrible knot in her stomach whenever she thought about her past, kept her stunned to the spot.

She forced her gaze on Kevin, easing her mind into the present. His thick hair had a hint of a curl she couldn't help but want to touch. His green eyes were warm and appeared to appreciate every tiny nuance of life around him. He was smiling, as he always was.

And he was a nurse.

What kind of man became a *nurse?*

Chapter Three

Mack jammed the bouquet of multicolored baby carnations into the porcelain vase he'd brought along with him and placed it square in the middle of the red-and-white plaid blanket he had laid on the floor of Abigail's bedroom. With a loud sigh, he sat back on his heels, folded his arms over his chest, and cocked an eyebrow at his handiwork.

Flower-themed paper plates, matching napkins and cups, and plastic utensils had been carefully and lovingly set up by his smiling little charge, whom he had gently placed down on a soft blanket next to the feast when she insisted on helping him. Her excitement rubbed off on him, and he felt jittery and young.

Along with the plates and napkins, Mack had brought along a wicker basket full of delectable picnic goodies from the deli. He had sweated over every detail; picnics weren't really his style.

This was the first he had planned, in fact, and he wanted everything to be perfect for Abby.

And Lily.

Hence the flowers in the fancy vase and the flower theme. He wanted to create a happy mood for the ladies. But now that he thought about it, he wasn't so sure they were such a good idea.

"So what do you think, Abby?" he asked, cupping his chin with one hand. "Tell me the truth. I promise I can handle it."

"Mom is gonna hate it," Abby confirmed with a cheerful laugh.

Mack groaned and jammed his fingers through his hair. "I was afraid of that."

Abby laughed again. "Don't worry, Mr. Kevin. It's a good idea. Don't let my mom ruin everything. She's sad about everything."

Her happy voice stopped him flat, and he gazed affectionately at the little girl who had been through so much and had survived with her spirit—and her child's pure faith—intact.

"It is a good idea, isn't it?" he asked as much to convince himself as to concede to the little girl. "We'll just have to convince her of that, won't we?"

"Convince who of what?" said a very wary-sounding Lily from behind his back. It sounded to Mack as if her defenses were already dauntingly in place, and it was going to take a battle to knock them down.

He stiffened. This wasn't exactly how he wanted to present his good-idea scenario. But he was going to have to make do.

He winked at Abby and stood, whirling around to grin at her mother, determination swelling in his chest when he saw her frown.

Thinking quickly, he whipped up the vase of flowers and presented the multicolored bouquet to Lily with a flourish, as if that was what he had planned all the time. "Why, Abby and I wanted to convince you to stop and smell the flowers, of course. What did you think?"

She accepted the vase he held before her, and to Mack's surprise, took a long whiff of the flowers. He wouldn't have thought her the flower type.

Maybe his idea wasn't so hopeless after all. Surprises lay behind every corner.

Her gaze met his. She didn't say anything, but her confused wide gaze told him exactly what she thought.

She was grateful for the gesture, but she didn't know what to make of *him*.

"Who sent the flowers?" she asked at last, sounding a little less suspicious.

A little.

Mack tried to speak, but no words came out of his mouth. He cleared his throat and started again. "I brought them. For you."

"You? For *me*? But…"

"Please don't argue, Mommy," Abby said, quickly

cutting off her mother's words. "The flowers are so pretty, don't you think?"

Lily whirled around with a yelp of surprise, her mouth dropping open and her hands flying to her hips, bouquet still in her grip. "Abigail Rose, what are you doing on the floor? There's a draft. You'll catch your death of cold!"

She spun around, then pierced Mack with her sharp gaze. "Mr. MacCormack, I don't know what you could have been thinking to have—"

"She's on a nice, thick blanket, Lily," he said calmly. "And you'll notice I've wrapped her in a sweater, so she won't be bothered by drafts," he pointed out, his voice thick as his throat tightened.

"I appreciate your thoughtfulness, but be that as it may, I don't think—"

"Then don't think, Lily," he said, interrupting her negative diatribe. "*Feel* for a couple of hours. I promise you will enjoy it."

He paused and winked. "I brought dessert."

Mack had to admit he was surprised when her beautiful brown eyes lit up. "Dessert?" she echoed. "Is it chocolate?"

He chuckled and took her by the arm, leading her to a seat by the picnic blanket. "Would I bring anything else to a pair of ladies? I may be a big lug of a man, but I know what women want."

She laughed. "Go on," she said, her voice taking on a sultry quality. "I'm listening."

"Eclairs. From a little specialty shop not too many people know about. Fluffy pastry, the best cream you've ever tasted." He paused, dangling his words over her like a carrot to a bunny. "And of course, rich, smooth chocolate smeared all over the top."

Lily laughed and held her hands up. "You had me at eclairs."

"Mom is a chocoholic," Abby gravely informed Mack as if that were an important fact he should take note of.

He grinned. "Don't worry, Abby, I don't think an addiction to chocolate is too high on the negative scale as things go."

Lily suddenly scowled at him, and he hadn't a clue what had changed her mood. But he was good and determined to change it back again.

"Just think, sweetie, it could be worse. She could get regular cravings for pickled herring." He tickled the little girl's tummy as he said the words, and she screeched and squirmed in response.

Mack glanced at Lily, who was apparently enjoying the interplay. Whatever had pushed her button a moment before appeared to have vanished now that she had accepted the idea of an unconventional picnic, in an unconventional place, with an unconventional guest serving the food.

"Mom, what's a herring?" Abby said when she could speak without laughing.

Lily's whole face lit up when she gazed at her daughter, and for the first time since Mack had known her, her smile was genuine. Her eyes were shining with love for her daughter, and her cheeks were flushed with unspoken emotion.

In that moment, he made a phenomenal discovery. Lily wasn't just a pretty Southern woman who could easily catch a man's eye with a turn of her head and a flick of her long black hair.

She was absolutely *beautiful*.

She took his breath clean away. He hoped she wouldn't ask him a question until he could regain his power of speech and be able to breathe at a marginally normal pace once again.

"A herring is a fish, darling." Lily stared at her daughter sprawled casually on the blanket and realized just what Nurse Kevin MacCormack and his crazy picnic had done for the little girl.

Abigail was smiling and her cheeks were full of color and vivacity.

Adora was adamant about keeping Abigail restricted to her bed now that she was in control of things. All the poor, injured girl could do with her time was color in books and hook rugs and watch cartoon reruns over and over. Things that would drive any sane seven-year-old girl crazy within a day.

Abigail was still afraid to face the outdoors, so Kevin had brought the outdoors to her. It was deeply sensitive, and it made her wonder about the man who was Abigail's official angel.

At the moment, the man in question was sprawled on his side, leaning on one muscular arm and looking completely relaxed and at ease with himself and the world.

"What's in the basket?" Lily asked, trying to distract herself from her own troublesome thoughts. She sat down, tucking her legs under her and straightening her spine, as her mother had taught her so many years ago. "Besides eclairs, I mean."

Kevin gave Abigail a conspiratorial wink and opened the wicker basket. "I've got goodies galore, and enough to feed an army. I'm sure you'll find something you like in here." He paused. "Besides eclairs, I mean," he said, echoing her words.

She rolled her eyes at him, but he got a good chuckle out of her.

He paused dramatically before continuing. "Bread," he said slowly, pulling out a circular loaf of shepherd's bread, which he followed with a tub of butter and a thick, curved silver butter knife.

Lily thought the bread must still be warm from the oven, because the tantalizing aroma of freshness tickled her nostrils. Her heart was beating rapidly in her throat, no matter how often she inwardly coaxed herself to calm down.

Kevin smiled softly, as if sensing her thoughts. "And of course I brought cheese to go with the bread." He pulled out a small tray containing a variety of flavors of cubed cheese, from sharp cheddar to mozzarella and everything in between. "Oh, and I picked up a pound of fresh strawberries, if anyone is interested. If not, I can always—"

"No!" Lily interrupted. "We love fresh strawberries, don't we, Abigail?"

Lily's mouth was watering, and she had to smile at the boyish eagerness on the face of the man doling out the goodies. His smile was certainly contagious, and she knew he was working his charm on Abigail as much as he was captivating her.

"Last, but certainly not least," Kevin continued, pausing long enough to meet both Abigail's eyes and then Lily's gaze, "we have the fried chicken."

Lily laughed out loud when Kevin pulled out a big bucket of fried chicken he had obviously purchased from a local fast-food restaurant.

"What?" he protested, his face all innocence and merriment. "We can't have a picnic without fried chicken, can we?"

"No," Lily agreed, "I suppose we can't." She still couldn't believe she was sitting on the carpeted floor of her daughter's room in her mother's mansion getting ready to eat something as messy and unrefined as fried chicken…and in the company of a handsome man.

Adora would have an apoplectic fit if she found out about this little stunt.

But Abigail had definitely perked up at the idea of a picnic, so how could Lily say no?

"Light or dark?" Kevin queried.

"What?" she responded absently, his deep voice yanking from her thoughts.

"Chicken. Light or dark meat?" he clarified with a chuckle. She saw that he had already given Abigail her favorite, a drumstick.

She cleared her throat, her brain oddly fuzzy. "Dark."

He handed her a thigh, took a large piece of white meat for himself, and buttered a piece of bread for each of them.

He continued to sprawl across one end of the blanket, still smiling. It made her nervous just watching him relax. He looked like a big cat after a large meal.

Before he started eating, he unfolded a napkin and tucked it into the top of his scrub shirt. Lily found the motion oddly endearing, and she fought a smile, knowing if Kevin saw it he would want an explanation for what she found so funny.

"Shall we pray?" Kevin asked offhandedly.

"Why, yes," Lily answered, thinking it would be rude to refuse such a request. She bowed her head and closed her eyes.

"Thank you, Lord, for food to strengthen us to do Your will, and friends to share it with. In Christ's holy name, Amen."

"Amen," Lily echoed thankfully. She had squirmed

through the whole short prayer. Kevin spoke with such grave reverence, and yet such loving fervency, that she wanted to get up and run away.

When was the last time she had thought to pray over her food? It must have been in childhood. She couldn't remember, and for some reason, that bothered her.

As Lily sat gracefully on the floor, still straight-backed and stiff as a rod, the day and the mood and the small talk with Kevin began to take effect.

Slowly, subtly, she felt the nervous tension sliding from her shoulders as she delicately bit into her first bite of chicken.

"Great picnic, huh, Mom?" Abigail asked over a mouthful of bread.

"Don't speak with your mouth full, dear," Lily corrected automatically, and Kevin chuckled. She gave him a direct look to remind him *she* was the parent here, and then turned to Abigail and said primly, "Yes, honey, it's a lovely picnic."

"And what a location," Kevin said, sounding as if he meant it. "Look, there's a little bird."

As he pointed high up on one wall, he pursed his lips and made an imitation of a robin's spring song that was so genuine Lily could almost believe it.

Abigail giggled.

"And there's a deer in that meadow over there." He nodded his head toward the dresser. "Do you see the rack on that thing? He must be king of all the bucks, leading the whole herd."

Kevin's gaze met hers, silently coaxing her into this game. Lily mentally scrambled to catch up to his wild way of thinking. She wasn't used to make-believe.

"Is that a bunny I see hopping across our picnic blanket? Oh, I hope he doesn't get his feet in the strawberries." Lily chuckled over her feeble attempt to fit into this game.

To her surprise and wonder, Abigail squealed with laughter, and she and Kevin soon joined into the contagion of her giggles.

"That bunny isn't going to step on the strawberries," Kevin assured her with a smile. "I'm guessing he'll eat the things before he tromps on them."

"Oh, good point," Lily agreed with a soft smile. "I stand corrected. But I do envy that horse running through the field."

"What kind of horse?" Kevin asked softly, leaning forward on his arm to meet her gaze.

"Oh, I don't know," she said. "A buckskin, I guess. But that's a color, not a type of horse."

"Good enough," he said, nodding his head. "Why don't you go over and see what kind of ride he gives you. You don't want a horse you can't ride."

"Oh, but I couldn't," Lily protested, shaking her head and placing a palm over her heart.

The ironic thing was that she wasn't protesting over

the fact Kevin had just asked her to ride an imaginary horse. No...

"You can't ride," guessed Kevin, reaching out to push back a stray strand of her hair. His fingers brushed her cheek. "Am I right?"

Lily looked away, effectively brushing away his hand. She didn't answer him. It was a dream of her life, a dream she'd never fulfilled, to go horseback riding.

"My mother insisted on ballet lessons," she explained, her voice crackling with emotion. "She thought horseback riding was too dangerous, even though all of my friends were doing it."

"And ballet?" he queried.

She really didn't want to talk about this, but Kevin seemed so genuine and honest she found herself blurting out the truth.

"I was awful. Really awful. Do *not* try to picture me in a tutu." She blushed after she said it.

"Don't worry. I'm picturing you on the back of a horse, galloping with the wind whipping your hair and the ground flying before you."

So was she. But it didn't help to think about such things. After a moment, she placed her best attempt at a smile on her face and tried to change the subject. "Do you think the elephant in the back corner will present us with a problem?"

Abigail held her stomach against the laughter. "Oh,

Mom, cut it out. Everyone knows there are no elephants in the woods."

Lily shrugged and swung her long black hair back over her shoulder. "If you say so, honey. But I'm telling you, I see an elephant in that corner. I see a problem in the working."

"Then we'd best pick up this food before he gets hungry," Kevin suggested. "I'd like to put Abigail back into her bed and check her vitals, and then I'll clean up my mess."

"*Your* mess?" Lily immediately protested. "How did this become your mess?" She chuckled and reached out her hand to graze him in the ribs.

He didn't laugh. In fact, he rolled so quickly onto his feet she almost would have thought his scrubs were on fire.

It was the first time she'd ever seen him genuinely frown, and it made her feel like curling into a ball and hiding.

"I'm not ticklish," he rasped. His voice wasn't harsh, but it was firm enough to let Lily know her advances weren't welcome.

She pulled in her emotions and continued through a tight throat. "We enjoyed this picnic every bit as much as you did, didn't we, Abigail?"

Abigail nodded. "And we made a big mess, too, didn't we, Mommy?"

"We're in agreement, then," Lily said, her voice strict

and businesslike, with no room for argument. "Kevin, you do whatever a nurse needs to do for my little Abigail, and I'll clean up here."

"Mom," Abigail complained. "Will you stop doing that?"

"What? Cleaning up?"

"No. Treating me like I'm a little kid. You're embarrassing me."

"What? No mention of her control issues?" Kevin murmured under his breath, effortlessly sweeping Abigail into his arms and holding her tight against his chest until he gently deposited her into bed.

Lily, in the process of picking up the paper plates, started to stand and whirl on him for his uncalled for, if admittedly accurate remark, but then she thought better of it.

If she started something now, she wouldn't be in control. She had to work her emotions into some kind of shape first, although right now she was mostly feeling numb, and a little hurt.

Resigned, she put the steam which would otherwise have escaped through her ears into quickly and efficiently cleaning up the picnic space. At least she had something practical to do.

Kevin's tone of voice had been joking, and she did know her own weaknesses, after all. She *had* taken over, ordering everyone to a task. Maybe it was her many years in the political arena, but her perfectionist, get-it-done attitude was every much a part of her as the heart beating in her chest.

And if he had some kind of problem being touched, well, it was his problem. Not hers. She shouldn't feel bad about it.

With everything put neatly back in its place, Lily moved to Kevin's side. He was standing over Abigail's bed, watching her sleep.

He chuckled softly as she approached and, putting a finger to his lips, gestured at the now-sleeping child curled up in the big white bed. "Enough excitement for one day, I guess."

Lily swallowed her flaring emotions and gave in to good Southern manners. She gently laid her hand on his arm, hoping he wasn't *that* touch-shy, and he turned toward her.

"I don't know how I can thank you," she said softly, and then realized that, for whatever it was worth, she meant it.

"For what? I'm just doing my job, Lily." His voice sounded oddly choked.

"That's not all you're doing, and you know it. I haven't seen Abigail smile so much since—" She stopped suddenly, her throat welling up so she could hardly speak. "Since—"

"Since the accident," Kevin finished for her, his deep voice low, kind and gentle.

"Well, I owe you one. And I always pay my debts, Kevin," she said fervently.

"Don't bother," he said, and this time, the tone of his voice sounded a little bit harsh.

She got the message. *Back off.*

For a moment, while she was lounging on the floor picnicking with Kevin, she felt like part of the world again. She'd felt connected to another human being, someone she could trust.

Obviously, she had been wrong.

Blinking rapidly, she cleared her throat, willing herself under control. She met his gaze directly, without letting one ounce of the turmoil she was feeling inside slip out. Whatever else might happen, he would never know how he'd gotten to her.

"So," she said mildly, even smiling a little, "what are we going to do about that elephant?"

Chapter Four

Quietly, though he knew he would not be overheard in the soundproof room, Mack leaned an arm on the two-way mirror that allowed him to keep silent watch over Abby, and then leaned his forehead against his forearm, as if that movement brought him closer to the poignant situation he was experiencing here at the Montague mansion.

He often found himself drawn to the window, especially after hours. Abby was as sweet as an angel when she was asleep. The month of pain the poor little child had experienced disappeared off her face, replaced by the soft look of childhood innocence that managed to choke up even a tough guy like Mack.

A fierce protective instinct arose in his chest at the sight of the sleeping girl. He had always been one of the good guys, fighting for justice and right.

But this situation had somehow become personal, though he was always meticulously careful to keep his emotions away from his job. Yet Lily and Abigail were no longer just his *assignment*—they had become a necessary part of his life.

Though he knew he would, by the same necessity, walk away and not look back when the job was done, he also knew he would carry a part of these two extraordinary females—and even of domineering Adora—with him when he left. They had changed his life forever, even if they would never know it.

No matter how tough an act Lily put on, she was vulnerable. He had seen that mark in her expression today when he'd backed away from her to keep his sidearm a secret.

It was only a brief flash of vulnerability before the mask she normally wore was fully into place, but it was more than enough to clue Mack in to the fact that her feelings ran deeper than she was letting on. She kept herself at such a distance, and then, there it was in her eyes—the truth.

He supposed he'd thought of Lily as he thought of her mother—dignified and aloof, one step above the rest of the world. Lily didn't smile often, except at Abby, and then only with a bittersweet twist of her lips.

He sighed softly and groaned into his arm. He'd always been the man who followed orders, who did the tough jobs no one else wanted.

Well, this was a *tough* job all right. The toughest he'd ever known. He was personally engaged in this mission to help Abby whether he liked it or not.

His breath came in a quick intake as Lily slipped quietly into Abby's room and moved with soft steps to the little girl's bed.

Mack closed his eyes for a moment, knowing he was an unwelcome intruder, invading a private moment. He knew he should turn around and walk away, busy himself cleaning his pistol or something, move his focus and concentration somewhere besides what was happening in the darkened room beyond the two-way mirror.

But he was just as frozen as if his arm was glued to the wall. No amount of internal struggle with his conscience could make him part from the view he saw when he opened his eyes, could keep him from watching Lily with her daughter.

Lily was kneeling beside Abby's bed, gently stroking her daughter's blond hair away from her forehead. It was a soft, rhythmic movement that lulled Mack into a sense of tranquility he supposed Abby, too, must be feeling, asleep and at peace with the world and God.

He swallowed hard as he watched the progress of Lily's fingers as she traced the line of her daughter's chin. It was only when he looked up and saw the single tear making a slow trail down Lily's cheek that he turned his face away, his jaw taut with anger.

A woman like Lily shouldn't have to face this kind

of agony, especially not alone. For the first time since he'd walked in the door of the mansion, he realized what utter horror she must be going through.

And with no one to turn to for love and comfort, no one to protect and cherish her.

As much as he was growing to love the little girl he cared for day in and day out in the two weeks he'd been there, how much more must her mother's agony be at the tragedy? He hadn't realized how she must be grieving over the accident that had put her sweet daughter in such terrible circumstances.

Yet he'd never seen a hint of what lay behind her facade until today. She always appeared to be the tower of strength, the one on whom everyone else leaned.

As an ex-army ranger, he'd been in more uncomfortable situations, even if he couldn't think of one at the moment—at least not one more emotionally uncomfortable.

The only way he could think of to undo the damage he'd done today with his boorish behavior was to go to Lily and explain why he'd been such an unfeeling and insensitive jerk.

Except he couldn't explain what was truly going on or why he had really turned her away when she'd tried to touch him.

Terrific.

He was really in trouble. For a man of honesty and integrity, firmly dedicated to upholding the Christian principles he believed in with all his heart, he was definitely treading on shaky ground.

"Lord Jesus," Mack muttered, straightening his hair with the tips of his fingers, *"granted, you were God, but you were also a man who was put in more than a few tight spots in your life on earth. Do you have any good suggestions for me right about now?"*

He chuckled, sure that his Lord had more than a few good suggestions and that Mack wasn't close to following anywhere near half of them.

Still, a little prayer couldn't hurt.

He didn't have the slightest clue what he was going to say or do when he saw Lily. All he knew was that he needed to make some sort of overture of friendship to her, and he needed to make it tonight.

He needed to keep his cover secure, but he needed to be on speaking terms with Lily, keeping the lines of communication open so she would confide in him if anything more developed with the case he should know about.

Beyond that, it was anyone's guess.

Deciding it wasn't going to get any easier with him standing there fiddling with his hair, he mumbled another short prayer for guidance and strode purposefully from the room.

He walked about three paces before making an abrupt halt.

This house was bigger than Mercury. Where was he

supposed to look for Lily? She'd left Abigail's bedroom more than an hour ago.

He traced a hand under his jaw and frowned. The logical place to start was her bedroom, but he was uncomfortable seeking her there. He decided to look elsewhere and save her private dwelling as a last-ditch effort.

He wandered through the drawing room and into the living room, but the rooms were large, empty and silent. It was difficult to keep his boots from making noise on the highly polished hardwood floor.

Every cushion, every knickknack had been perfectly placed, with careful thought to the decor. It was more than a living room, it was a statement.

It was artwork.

And it said a lot about the esteemed Adora Montague. She did not leave anything to another's care. Instead, she put her own heart into what she did.

And yet there was a great expanse of emptiness to the room, as well. The house was so big, it was something even Adora Montague could not escape, he realized with a spine-tingling straightness.

He swallowed hard and continued his quest.

The dining room was likewise sterile, the table immaculate with a white lace cloth and the sideboard filled with gleaming sterling silver. Nothing but the very best for Mrs. Montague. The best silver, the best furniture, the best art from the most famous of artists to hang on her walls.

Why would Lily give all this up? Why had she left so abruptly and gone out on her own? He only knew that she'd been very young when she left, and that she hadn't returned to the mansion until now.

He had heard the story, but he would bet his next paycheck didn't know the whole story. And for some reason, he very much wanted to know. The facts were plain. Lily's husband, David Larson, an FBI special agent, died in the line of duty, leaving Lily to raise their unborn child alone. And just when she'd worked her way up, and had created a stable home for Abby, Senator Mc-Cain's son Jeremy had been kidnapped from the playground of a private school. In the tussle, Abby had been trampled by the kidnappers, which left her paralyzed physically and emotionally. But now it seemed the kidnappers were trying to finish the job they'd started and ensure the permanent silence of the little girl who could identify them.

But though the situation was bad, it was the emotion lurking beneath the surface that most disturbed Mack.

He generally wasn't the type of guy who snooped into other people's private lives, especially not on the job. But Lily was far too intriguing. He couldn't help but to want to know more about her. She fascinated him in a way he couldn't begin to explain.

He peeked into the kitchen hoping she was making herself a snack, but, not surprisingly, was disappointed to find the room as empty as the others had been.

Pin-droppingly quiet. Stiffly immaculate. Pristine to a fault.

He sighed deeply. He was going to have to visit her bedroom and see if she was there. Frowning, he shook his head. This wasn't the 1800s. And he was a gentleman. He would simply knock on the door and see what happened. Any other guy wouldn't be struggling with this.

Except he knew how Lily felt.

And he respected those feelings, those wishes that remained unsaid but were clear nonetheless.

But he had to breach that line in order to make things right between them. And if it took knocking on her bedroom door to do so, then so be it.

But first, he was going to get a breath of fresh air and clear his head. He walked back through the kitchen and slipped through the patio door in the dining room, sliding it quietly shut and strolling softly into the well-kept English-style garden.

The cool air swept across his face and smoothed his sweat-stained forehead. He hadn't even realized he was that tense. He wiped his forehead with the back of his thumb and chuckled. He'd heard his pals at work going on about their women problems, but he'd never experienced anything like this.

He walked farther into the garden, taking deep breaths and trying mentally to regroup. All this over a woman and a gun.

Go figure.

Suddenly he heard a noise.

He froze, all his training instantly coming into play. There shouldn't be someone in the garden at this time of night, and despite the fact he knew Adora's security system was state-of-the-art, he stealthily went on full alert against a possible intruder.

Lily walked stiffly across the brick garden path. She'd thought, after seeing Abigail sleeping, that a walk in the cool air would do her good, but the humidity felt stifling and choking.

Or maybe it was just her circumstances choking the life out of her. She never remembered feeling so miserable, not even after David died.

Abigail deserved so much better than what little Lily could give her. The dear child's faith in God was so strong, her hope so steadfast, while Lily's own weakhearted faith had departed long ago.

She'd searched and searched for Him, but God had deserted her.

And yet He was all around her.

Kevin was clearly a man of faith. His Abigail-proclaimed guardian-angelship aside, he often recited clearly beloved Bible stories when Abigail was close to sleeping, prayed along with her to a loving and precious Savior when she was scared, and played zippy games of Bible trivia with his sharp and rambunctious patient to keep her from getting bored.

Even Adora had her more formal, liturgical worship that took her off to church every Sunday morning with her Bible and prayerbook and was a well-cemented part of her life.

Lily shivered, though the evening was not especially chilly, and she had thought to put on a sweater before she made the trek out into the garden.

She longed for comfort. She desperately wanted the internal warmth of the fire only God could give to her heart.

And for the first time since David had died, she longed, really longed, for a man's arms around her. She ached to feel the strength of a man's arms bonded tightly to her and promising warmth and protection, if only for a little while.

She didn't know if the sudden vision of Kevin gently holding her was because of what had happened today, or because of some mixed-up emotions roiling through her, or because he was the only man in the vicinity.

She laughed aloud at the thought.

"What's so funny?"

Lily screamed in surprise and whirled around to face the voice behind her, though she recognized the rich, deep bass.

"Didn't your mother ever teach you not to sneak up on people?" she demanded, cocking her hands on her hips and glaring at him.

Kevin blinked and stepped back. Even in the moonlight she saw him blanch and then turn a healthy shade of red. His throat worked as if he was having difficulty swallowing.

After a moment he appeared to regain his equilibrium, sliding his expression into a neutral mask, though, Lily noted with a hint of satisfaction, his face was still scarlet.

"Actually, I've been professionally trained to sneak up on people," he said, his voice unusually low and deep as he chuckled at his own joke. "I guess I'm better at it than I realized."

"Oh, I see. What kind of college did you attend? Along with anatomy and physiology you studied creeping around in the dark startling people? That's a useful skill for a nurse."

She paused and shook her head. "Coming like a thief in the night is supposed to be Jesus's business, not yours, Kevin MacCormack."

"I didn't mean to startle you." His eyes were glimmering in the darkness. "I'm sorry. I was deep in thought, but I should have been paying more attention to where I was going."

She chuckled and shook her head. "No permanent harm done. I didn't suffer a heart attack, although if I were to, I supposed being in the presence of a nurse is as good a place as any."

He ran a hand across his jaw and chuckled along with her, eyeing her as if to figure out what she was really up to. "Please, no more patients. I've got enough on my plate getting Abby well again."

Lily wrapped her arms around herself and turned away from him so he wouldn't see the emotions she knew were flitting across her face.

He had made a simple statement of fact. It wasn't his fault his words were like daggers to her heart.

"I misspoke," he said gruffly. "Lily, you have to know I would never intentionally do or say anything to hurt you."

She stiffened as his palms settled warmly and gently on her shoulders. His touch was oddly comfortable, but at the same time unnerving, and Lily shrugged away, walking in what she hoped was a calm and not-too-hurried manner toward the gazebo in the middle of the garden, hoping he would take the hint and leave.

He didn't.

"Don't run away from me, Lily," he called after her. "We have some unfinished business between us. We need to talk."

"I accept your apology," she tossed over her shoulder, unconsciously quickening her pace as she neared the gazebo steps.

"That's nice, but that's not what I'm talking about." His voice was disturbingly close behind her, and she chanced a quick glance backward.

He was evidently following her to the gazebo.

She walked faster. "I came out to the garden tonight to be alone." If the man wasn't going to respond to subtlety, she would lay the facts out for him in straight order.

"Don't worry," he said softly from deep in his throat. "I'll leave."

She felt a pang of remorse for speaking so bluntly, but knew in her heart she'd done the right thing for both of them. It was better, she'd learned, to keep a healthy distance between people, and though Kevin appeared to want to be her friend as well as her mother's employee, she could not let that happen. She could not risk opening her heart to anyone.

"I'll leave," he said again. "After we talk."

Her breath left her lungs in a whoosh of shock and surprise. By this time she had reached the gazebo stairs, and she marched up them quickly before turning around to face the scurrilous nurse chasing her down as if in a fox hunt.

She sighed deeply. "Kevin, it's been a long day. Please, just go away."

A deep chuckle emerged from his chest. "You'd like that, wouldn't you, Lily?"

He took the steps two at a time and was at her side the next moment. Clouds must have covered the moon, for the gazebo was suddenly shrouded in darkness and shadows.

Lily shivered. All she could see was the feral gleam of Kevin's eyes. He was after something, and her hair stood on end when she realized she was the prey in question.

"You hold everyone at arm's length," he said, stepping forward so she had no choice but to step back. "Why is that, I wonder?"

He stepped forward again, and she stepped backward until she felt one of the solid posts of the gazebo pressing solidly against her back. She had nowhere left to run.

To escape.

"I have no idea what you're talking about," she said, swallowing hard when he quickly closed the distance between them, taking advantage of his position by placing his arms on either side of her head.

His muscular arms were as effective as the steel bars of a jail cell. Lily had always known Kevin was a handsome man, but now, a shadow in the darkness, he towered larger than life.

She could feel his warm breath on her cheek, yet he didn't speak. He was staring at her as if he was trying to read her, trying to figure out what made her tick. It seemed he wanted to know what she was thinking.

Well, just let him try. She stared back with more boldness than she was feeling. She couldn't tell from his expression what he was thinking, so she supposed they were on even terms in that respect.

She only knew that once she had locked gazes with him, she couldn't break herself away. She stared back at him as if in a trance.

He slanted his head and his green eyes gleamed

through the darkness. He smiled and leaned in ever so slightly, closing the distance between them slowly and effectively.

Lily pushed backward as hard as she could, but the post was not budging.

She was afraid that she was about to be kissed. And she didn't know whether she was disconcerted because she didn't want him to kiss her, or because she did.

With a quiet sigh, she closed her eyes and leaned her head back on the post, emotionally resigning herself to the inevitable. Let Kevin kiss her if he wanted to. She would decide how she felt about it later, when she was alone in her own room.

She waited and waited and waited for the touch of his lips on hers, but it never came.

With his thumb, he gently stroked a line across her cheek and underneath her chin. With his hand smooth against her jaw, he tilted her head forward and whispered, "Lily, open your eyes."

She wanted to squeeze her eyes as tightly shut as possible, but against her better judgment, she followed his request and opened her eyes, forcing herself to meet his warm gaze.

"You're not alone," he said, continuing to stroke her cheek with his thumb.

"What?" she asked, confused. Whatever she'd expected him to say, this wasn't it.

"You do everything by yourself," he explained gently. "You think the weight of the whole world's problems are solely yours to bear on your shoulders with no help whatsoever, don't you?"

"I haven't the slightest idea what you mean," she snapped back defensively. "I haven't exactly had an easy life, thank you very much."

"No," he agreed immediately. "You haven't."

His empathetic gaze backed up the sympathy and tenderness in his voice. "Which is why it's so tragic you feel you're all alone."

Lily's breath was coming sharply, and tears burned in the corners of her eyes. What was he trying to do, make her break down completely?

"You're not alone," he repeated, his hands moving to her shoulders as if he would shake his message into her. But he didn't shake her.

"You have your mother. You have Abigail. She worries about you, you know."

Lily nodded and stared at the expanse of his chest. He was rock-solid through and through, yet he was the gentlest man she had ever known.

He used his index finger to tip her chin upward so she was looking directly into his eyes. "And," he continued, his voice soft now, "now you have me."

His voice was so rich with tenderness she could hold back no longer.

With a sharp cry, she stepped into the warmth and strength of his arms and began sobbing. He wrapped his arms tightly around her, stroked her hair, and murmured sweet words softly in her ear.

She clung to him, her fists closing around the soft cotton of his T-shirt. She hadn't cried since the day she'd left her mother's house at age eighteen.

She hadn't cried at the death of her husband David, or even after Abigail's tragedy. She had had to be the strong one then, she had convinced herself, and crying made a person weak.

But right here, right now, Kevin was the strong one, and Lily was surprised at the strength of her emotions. It was only after several minutes that she quieted her tears and stood emotionally drained and spent in Kevin's solid embrace.

"I'm sorry," she apologized. "I don't normally—that is, I can't imagine what came over me."

Kevin let out a low groan. "I can, Lily. And please don't ever apologize for being human."

She wiped her wet cheeks with her palms and turned sideways in his grasp, an obvious attempt to escape his hold on her.

He let her go.

She didn't like feeling vulnerable, and that's what crying had done for her. Stepping out of Kevin's arms only enhanced the feeling.

But she felt better, too.

The pain and awful heaviness she'd carried in the deep, dark recesses of her soul for so many years was gone. She felt lighter, cleaner somehow, as if the tears had washed away the many years of sorrow she'd kept hidden inside her.

"Thank you," she offered tentatively, not daring to look at him.

"Anytime," he replied back promptly.

She started to walk back to the house, wanting the solace of her room to consider what had just happened to her.

"Lily?" Kevin called softly. This time, his voice sounded farther away. At least he wasn't following her, though she had mixed feelings even about that. She'd never been more confused in her life.

She stopped but did not turn around. "Yes?"

"I meant it." He said intensely, then paused. "Anytime."

Lily resumed her course toward the house, her heart beating rapidly though she was not walking all that fast. It was just one more reaction to a very crazy, bewildering day, and she ignored it.

Still, she couldn't help but think about what Kevin had said to her.

Why did she suppose she might just have to take him up on his offer?

Chapter Five

What had he been thinking?

Never a deep sleeper, Mack was up before dawn, pacing his room like a caged cat, every so often jamming his fingers into his hair or scrubbing his palm up and down the back of his neck.

He could have blown this case wide open. And try as he might, he couldn't find it within himself to completely regret it.

He'd wanted to kiss Lily last night, when the shadowy cast of the moonlight and the scent of her musky perfume mixed into a toxic sensation.

He wondered if she knew.

Probably not.

He'd practically stalked the poor woman in the garden last night, and he'd certainly not given her a choice whether or not to step into his embrace. If she did think about the two of them kissing in the moonlight, it probably wasn't any romantic notion she was harboring.

She had explicitly told him to leave, and instead he had forced a confrontation that had ended with Lily clinging to him, sobbing in his arms. That she had needed the moment, the opportunity to let everything go, was far beyond the point of the matter.

He worked for Adora, at least as a facade, and he could well imagine what the old woman would say if she found out about what had happened in his midnight rendezvous with Lily.

When she found out, he corrected himself.

Lily would no doubt have already approached her mother about firing the overbearing nurse who took advantage of a woman's weak emotional state.

And he probably should be fired, now that he thought about it.

At least his bag was already packed. He'd never gotten out of the habit of living out of a suitcase, even on an extended job like this one. He could zip and clip right out of there this morning, if that became necessary, which he desperately hoped would not be the case.

Deciding that thinking about the upcoming confrontation with Adora, and possibly Lily herself, was worse than actually doing it, he straightened his pale-green scrub shirt over his shoulder holster and set out to find the women.

He was halfway down the hallway when he suddenly

glanced at his watch. No one would be up to confront. He had at least four more hours to pace before Adora rose for the day.

He made it an agonizing three-and-a-half hours before he couldn't stand it anymore. With a throaty growl, he set off to find Adora and face the music.

Ironically, he found her at the piano in the formal living room, playing a graceful concerto with the ease of years of practice. She lifted her head to make eye contact with him without losing a single note.

As she finished, he stood stiffly with his legs braced apart and his hands behind his back, his stance a natural throwback from his years in the army. It was as comfortable as he was going to get until the older woman deigned to speak to him.

"Good morning, Mrs. Montague," he said as she rested her hands in her lap and looked up at him expectantly. He was glad now for his training, which kept the shake out of his voice and his expression calm and neutral, though he was anything but calm and composed on the inside.

He'd faced international terrorists with less stress than he was feeling at this moment. He couldn't believe the waves of emotion crashing through him like a tidal wave.

"Good morning, Mr. MacCormack."

When she didn't say anything else, sweat broke out on his forehead and he cleared his throat.

"Is there something I can do for you?" she asked after a long, agonizing moment.

His gaze narrowed on her, but she looked, as always, completely relaxed and in control.

And she looked as if she had no idea whatsoever why he was here.

Had Lily not run to her mother?

It was hard to conceive. He'd stepped far beyond his boundaries last night. Could it be true? Was he to have more time to find out who Lily really was inside, beyond the blatant facade she used to keep everyone at arm's length?

Had she kept what happened last night a secret between the two of them?

Lily answered the question herself when she strode into the room, fresh from the shower, her hair still wet and her cheeks blooming rose.

"Good morning, mother. Mr. MacCormack, how are you today?"

She bowed her head then, but not before he caught the wisp of a smile on her face and the healthy glow on her cheeks, the unusual brightness of her eyes.

He saw emotion in those dark depths. He didn't know *what* emotion, but compared to her usual stony stare, this revelation was like Christmas morning for Mack.

"Am I interrupting something?" she asked, looking at her mother and then at Mack, who still held his military posture.

"No, not at all," Mack answered immediately. "In fact, I was just on my way to see Abby. Would you like to walk with me?"

She looked startled for a moment, but then smiled softly. "I suppose that would be fine, Kevin. Just let me grab a muffin."

Adora lifted an eyebrow at Lily's use of his first name. It was a breach of Southern etiquette for Lily to be so informal, but the older woman didn't say anything about it, nor did she reprimand Lily in his presence, as he was sure Adora might usually have done. Lily had said enough that he had a good clue as to the relationship between mother and daughter.

He was glad he was here to stall the moment, and especially glad when Lily took his arm and tugged him toward Abigail's living quarters. Especially when she didn't let go of his arm as they walked down the long hallway.

"How is our little patient doing?" she asked as they walked. "I was just on my way to check on her, when I heard you and my mother talking."

Mack immediately perceived what she was doing— avoiding the intimacy of the prior evening with small talk. With her words she was subtly but firmly pushing him away, creating an invisible but unmistakable barrier between them.

He sighed inwardly, but put his hand over hers as it rested on his arm. At his touch she tried to pull away, but he wouldn't allow her, continuing to walk as if nothing was amiss.

"Abby's doing better than expected. She's tough and highly motivated, just like her mother. She's fighting with everything in her little heart to get well, and I think in time she will."

He turned to see Lily swipe at a tear. Apparently, he'd done it again. He had a knack for the impossible—making tough-minded Lily Montague shed tears.

He squeezed her hand to let her know he was there for her, even though he couldn't say the words he wanted to say.

After a moment, she not only relaxed, but tightened her grip, sliding her hand to rest securely on his upper arm.

"Do you think—" Lily faltered and then stopped, looking away from him.

He waited a moment for her to gain her composure, if not to complete her question, but he already knew what she was asking, even if she didn't voice it, and when she continued to stare at the opposite wall as they walked, he decided to prod ahead with the conversation on his own and put her at ease.

He was supposed to be Abby's nurse, after all. At least he could fill that role for Lily.

"At this point, Abby has physically healed, for the most part. I believe the battle she's waging in her mind is much worse than what happened to her body."

"The kidnapping," Lily said, her voice sounding choked and teetering on the edge of control.

"Precisely." He stopped and took in a ragged breath of his own. "You've got to understand I'm doing the best I can for her. I'm a nurse, not a psychologist, and I won't pretend to be. But I think the mental trauma she went through is as much to blame for her current condition as anything she endured physically when the perp—er—kidnapper ran her over. Her therapist agrees with me."

He glanced to see if she'd caught his foolish slip of the tongue. Once again he'd put his mission in jeopardy with his big mouth. He'd never had this trouble before, and he didn't know why it was suddenly so difficult for him to keep his personal life separate from his work.

When Lily made no reference to his slip-up, he breathed an inner sigh of relief and let himself relax a bit, smiling at Lily when they made eye contact.

One thing was clear—he was going to have to be more careful around her. For some reason, he'd discovered a vulnerable spot in himself when he was with Lily—somewhere in the neighborhood of his heart.

And it was coming out his mouth. He pinched his lips together as if that mere action would keep dangerous words from tumbling off his tongue.

They had reached the door to Abby's bedroom when Lily stopped suddenly, pulling him back from the child's door and into a small windowed niche tastefully decorated with a small bench and a variety of hanging plants. Sunshine poured in through the window, giving the nook a soft, romantic look.

Mack eyed the bench, but didn't think it would hold his weight, so he leaned a shoulder against the nearest wall and waited for Lily to speak.

She brushed her palms together and then clasped her hands in front of her. When she met his gaze, she was back to the calm, composed woman he'd grown to know. The woman in the iron mask.

"Tell me the truth, Kevin. I have to know."

A moment of panic overwhelmed him, until he understood she wasn't asking for his state secrets. She was referring to Abby.

He ran his tongue across his bottom lip, gauging just how much he should tell her, wondering what exactly she was asking of him. She didn't break his gaze, but challenged him with her warm brown eyes.

"I think, with time, Abby will recover fully and be a normal child again."

"She'll walk again?" There was neither surprise nor excitement in her statement.

He wished he could reassure her. He wished he could tell her what she wanted to hear. He wanted to have the ability to walk into Abby's bedroom and snap his fingers to make her whole again.

"It would help Abby to have a child psychiatrist.

Maybe if we hooked up with the FBI…" he suggested tentatively.

"No!"

Her response was so quick and so vehement Mack took a step backward, crossing his arms to keep from the natural instinct to hold his hands up in front of him.

Lily's face had darkened and rage gleamed in her eyes. "No FBI," she snapped harshly and turned toward the window, hugging her arms around her.

"Lily?" Mack said.

Adora had briefed him on how Lily's husband David had been killed in the line of duty for the FBI. How he hadn't even known Lily was pregnant with Abby. It was no wonder bitterness oozed from the woman at the very name of the secretive government agency.

The agency he worked for.

He knew he ought to leave it be. He didn't like it when people pried into his personal affairs, and Lily was a very private woman. But for some reason, he wanted—needed—her to tell him because she wanted to. He wanted to hear it from *her* mouth.

So he asked. But he knew Lily. He didn't expect an answer.

To his surprise, she answered at once, her voice once again composed and even as she spoke. "My late husband was FBI."

"I see," he said, his throat tightening over the small words.

She whirled around, her eyes wide and accusing. "Do you?"

"W-well," he stammered, "I meant I sympathize with you. I'm sorry for your loss. It must have been very hard on you."

"But you think I'm stupid for not using FBI help now," she said through gritted teeth.

"I didn't say that," he protested.

"You're thinking it," she snapped back, narrowing her gaze on him. Then she clapped a hand over her mouth, looking mortified.

Still leaning on the wall, he merely stood and waited for what would come next.

"Kevin, I'm sorry. I can't believe how childish that sounded. The subject upsets me, but that's not an excuse for taking my bad feelings out on you. I apologize for my immature behavior."

Lily knew she was flushing with embarrassment and humiliation at her childish words, but Kevin quickly made it right again.

"You're forgiven," he said softly.

From any other man, Lily would have suspected those words to carry the edge of sarcasm or derision, and would have been suspicious.

But not from Kevin. He was the sweetest, most honest and open man she'd ever known, and she realized she inherently trusted him, even with family secrets. He'd entered the mansion that first day and somehow almost instantly had become part of the family, not just a mere employee.

"I won't pry," he said gently, reaching for her hand, "but have you ever talked to someone about it?"

She gave a short, cynical laugh. "Professionally, you mean? You think I need a shrink?"

Kevin looked appalled, and he dropped her hand immediately. His mouth opened and closed a few times before he spoke. "No, I never meant—"

"I know," she said, genuinely laughing as she let him off the hook. "I was teasing you."

"Oh," he said, sounding as confused as he looked. He had a little-boy vulnerability in his expression that Lily found attractive. "I was asking if you had talked to a friend or someone. Your mother?"

Lily shook her head. "Definitely not my mother, although she knows most of my sour story by default, especially when I had to move in here to hide from the kidnappers with Abigail in case they tried to come after her."

"A friend?" he suggested.

"I don't have any," she admitted softly.

"I don't believe that."

She made a garbled sound from her throat. She'd never been so mortified in her life. "Well, you'd better believe it. All I've ever done is work and take care of Abigail. I have acquaintances, but no real friends. No one I trust, anyway."

"What about church?" he asked. "I mean, before you went into hiding," he qualified with a sharp shake of his head. "Did you have a priest or pastor you could speak to about your situation?"

She looked him straight in the eye. "God and I aren't on speaking terms."

His eyes widened and he shifted from foot to foot. "That must be difficult for you," he said after a long pause.

"I live with it," she replied vaguely, waving him off with her hand. The jolt of the lie rocked her.

Of all that had changed in her life, her relationship with God—or rather, the lack of one—was what she most missed. She just didn't know how to go about making things right.

With God—or with anyone else in her life, for that matter.

Kevin didn't answer her directly, but she could see the kindness and sympathy in his eyes, and she knew he cared.

Truly cared.

And that was the one chink in her armor. She couldn't handle caring and kindness. So she started talking a mile a minute, hoping to dispel the rage of emotions swirling like a tornado in her chest.

"I never liked that David carried a gun," she began, determined Kevin would hear the whole sordid story. Then she would see how he felt, even if he couldn't really understand.

"I know I'm only one of a million wives of agents

and police and military men who pack heat as part of their jobs, but it never sat right with me. I worried all the time, and in the end, my concerns were verified. I was never meant to be an FBI agent's wife."

Kevin nodded and made a polite noise to let her know he was listening, but he didn't interrupt.

"I didn't mind being alone at night, or even those times when he was gone for weeks. I've always been pretty independent, so I just went my way and patiently waited for David to show up."

Kevin chuckled.

"Then came the day David was part of a team breaking a major meth lab thought to be the headquarters of a drug lord they'd been after for years."

She stopped and took a deep breath. She looked away for a minute, staring out the window, but then turned back and met Kevin's gaze. "There was a meth lab, but no drug lord. It was a setup."

Kevin visually tensed, his hands working into fists at his sides. She could see he understood the implications of what she said.

"David stumbled on a pipe bomb. The shrapnel killed him, hopefully instantly, as the FBI told me later. I've had nightmares about him suffering."

"Aw, Lily," Kevin groaned, and pulled her into his arms for a hug. "I'm so sorry."

"The worst part," she said, pushing away from him, determined not to break down and knowing she would if she stayed in his arms, "was that the same day I learned I was pregnant with Abigail."

Kevin shook his head, his mouth pinched tight. Now he was the one looking away, out the window.

"We had been trying to have a baby for over two years. We thought maybe we couldn't have children."

She paused, gathering her emotions. "And then when it finally happened—" She let the end of her sentence drop and she looked down at the carpet, struggling to regain her composure. It was harder to talk about than she had imagined it would be.

"You've had a rough go of it," Kevin said softly, his voice gruff with emotion and his expression sympathetic. "I promise I will do everything I can to make things easier for you from now on."

Lily's chuckle was full of emotion. "You already do, Kevin. Abigail wasn't far off when she called you an angel. You've been a real blessing to the whole family, and I know we couldn't get along without you now that we've had you around for a while."

She smiled when his face reddened under her scrutiny. She decided to strengthen her advantage.

"Now why didn't I marry a man like you?" she said in her best Southern-belle voice.

Kevin cleared his throat and stood up from where he'd been leaning, staring down at her in amusement, his eyes glimmering.

"And what kind of man would that be?" He was

squeezing his knuckles again, as if he was steeling himself for her answer, yet his face held a wide smile and his gaze was clear.

"Why, the best sort, of course. Kind, soft-spoken, sensitive—"

"Stop, stop already," he protested, holding out his hands palms out. "You make me sound like a total wimp. I'm no softie."

"Ri-i-i-ght," she agreed with a laugh.

He flexed his pecs. "I'm a man's man," he said in his lowest voice. "The world shudders when I walk by, and other men run for cover."

Lily was now laughing in earnest, her hand across her aching abdomen. "You know, not every woman longs for a callous brute for a husband."

He became instantly alert, his expression turning grim. "David never—"

Lily shook her head. "Oh no. Nothing like that. David did his best to be a good husband. I just discovered a little too late I don't really care for the rough-and-tough types."

When Kevin didn't respond, she continued. "I mean, look at you. You're a nurse. You help people with kindness and compassion instead of constant danger and the use of firearms."

He raised an eyebrow. "You know you do wonders to a man's ego. If you don't watch out, I'll be showing up in hot-pink scrubs one morning."

"And you'll be just as confident as ever," Lily assured him, rubbing her palm against his forearm. "Now, what do you say we go in and see how our little patient is faring?"

Mack couldn't have thought of a better idea. A minute more, and he was going to confess.

He hadn't been kidding when he'd told Lily he was a man's man, but even a tough guy would break under the scrutiny of the beautiful woman by his side.

Or the guilt.

Especially the guilt. She had no idea her every word was a hot poker into his soul.

A quiet, sensitive nurse? The guys at the bureau would have a heyday with that one.

Mack, who always took the tough jobs and never backed down. Mack, who was strong and silent only when it served his purpose.

He wondered, as he gave Abigail her morning physical, what might happen if he really was who he was pretending to be.

Might there be hope for some kind of a relationship with Lily? Could their friendship grow into something he had hardly dared to dream of, a relationship that would last forever?

Mack knew that wasn't for him. He'd made his decisions long ago, and he was too far down the path to turn around now.

But he'd never met a woman like Lily, a woman who shook the very core of everything he believed in.

And she hated him.

Or at least she would when she found out who—*what*—he was.

Everything she described about what she hated—every last bit of it—portrayed him to the letter, and he knew it. From head to toe, Mack knew he was Lily's worst nightmare come to life.

But she didn't have to know that, did she?

Once again that strange twinge of guilt pierced through him when he thought of his deception. He reminded himself again it was his duty, a part of his job he could not ignore.

And his deception was keeping little Abby—and her mother—safe. He must never forget that fact.

He needed to keep doing what he was doing, including the deception and the lies. He needed to keep Lily at arm's length so he didn't make a mistake.

Their lives might well depend on his ability to do his job and keep it a secret.

His confusion cleared as he thought rationally through the whole situation. He was letting his emotions dictate the pace, and he knew better than that.

If he kept working with Abby and praying with all his might, she could recover, Lord willing. And when she was emotionally healed, she would tell him what she knew about that day on the school playground, information that would, he hoped, save the life of another young child.

And then he could go away without ever revealing his true identity. Lily would always think of him as the gentle-hearted nurse who spent a few months caring for her ailing daughter.

And nothing more.

Chapter Six

Mack sat motionless on his cot, his back against the wall. He should have been asleep. But he was not sleeping, though it was nearly midnight and he had to be up early in the morning.

He was staring at the monitors that lined the other wall of his small quarters, the cameras that kept vigil on all the different parts of the property.

Nothing was moving, not on any of the cameras, even to Mack's trained eye. But he couldn't stop the notion that something somewhere on the grounds was not right. It was a sixth sense he'd developed over his time at the agency, the peculiar prickle at the back of his neck that told him danger was near.

He trusted his instincts.

Perhaps the grounds were too silent. Maybe it was the very fact nothing was moving that kept Mack on edge, his adrenaline pumping. He couldn't put his finger on it, but something was definitely wrong.

He was armed and ready. No one was going to hurt this family, not while he was in the picture. They had suffered enough already.

He stood suddenly and moved to one of the monitors, which had suddenly blacked out. Mack punched in some numbers on the keyboard but could not get the security system to respond.

He pinched his lips as he checked the other monitors, noting where the breach was located. He would have to hurry if he was going to intercept whoever it was before they reached the house.

If he calculated right, the perpetrators were headed straight through the garden to the glass veranda doors, the easiest to break or pick through. They had obviously cased the place.

Mack knew one more thing for certain—these men were experts. It wasn't easy to black out a portion of Adora's complex, state-of-the-art security system. Only the good guys and the crooks had that kind of knowledge to use for their purposes, and he wasn't thinking of the common thief, either.

Pulling his pistol from the holster, he moved over to the other side of the small room and leaned against the wall, pushing the small red button he had hoped never to have to use, the button that silently slid the two-way mirror open and allowed him quick access to Abby in an emergency.

At the same time he regretted the move, he thanked God for the foresight to make a quick, safe getaway possible for the little girl.

In a moment he was beside Abby's bed, bundling the girl into a blanket and into his arms. In another few seconds he'd slipped back behind the safety of the mirror. He felt rather than saw the door close behind him, and gave an internal sigh of relief.

One family member was safe, anyway.

He looked down to find Abby awake and eyeing him with a wide, sleepy gaze.

Or rather, she was eyeing the gun he still carried in his hand. He opened his mouth to reassure her, but no words followed.

It was only then he realized the little girl did not look frightened. Curious, perhaps, at seeing a gun close up, but not afraid.

Abby was a smart child. She knew what this meant; she was in danger.

But she didn't appear worried. After a moment, she sighed and laid her head against his chest. He could feel the slow rhythm of her breath, and concentrated on slowing his own, a difficulty when his heart was beating so rapidly.

He stroked Abby's hair for a moment, and then laid her on his cot and covered her up with his wool blanket, brushing her hair back and placing a gentle kiss on her forehead. "I'm going to have to leave you alone for a few minutes. Can you be brave for me?"

She looked around the room, at all the monitors and blinking lights, and then at Mack. After a moment, she nodded.

"That's a good girl. I just have to find your mother and grandmother and bring them here to this room. You are safe here, Abigail. This room is well-hidden. Here, I can protect you all. But I have to find your mother and grandmother."

Abby nodded again and snuggled into the blanket Mack had wrapped around her. When she closed her eyes, Mack made a swift exit into one of the house's long, claustrophobic hallways.

To his surprise, Adora was limping in his direction, her heels and her cane clacking loudly on the hardwood floor. The way her gray eyebrows creased above her nose let Mack know she wasn't coming for a social visit.

"I'll take care of Abigail," she said before he had the opportunity to speak. "You need to find Lily. I went by her room on my way here and she is not there. I cannot imagine where she would be at this time of night."

Mack wondered whether Adora was more perturbed that her carefully laid plans had been foiled, or if the high pitch to her voice was concern for her daughter. It looked like the monitor Adora also kept in her room had tipped her off.

"I think I know where to look," he assured her, his extensive training finally kicking in and giving him a calm heart and a cool head. He used his words to assure the older woman, then escorted her to his small safe house and the sleeping girl on his cot.

"There's a cell phone in that bag over there," he instructed Adora tersely, pointing to his black duffel bag. "Call for backup."

The older woman straightened her back from her precarious perch on the edge of the cot next to the sleeping Abby. She frowned and lifted her head, looking down her nose at him even though he was standing a good two feet over her. "I have already called for backup, young man. Now go find my daughter before she gets herself into trouble."

Both eyebrows raised in surprise at Adora's thoroughness and clear mind, he said the only thing he could think of to say.

"Yes, ma'am."

He slipped out of the room before she could give him additional orders. What he didn't need was Adora meddling in this operation.

"God, be with them," he prayed under his breath as he tucked into a military posture and ran full throttle through the expansive mansion. *"And especially with Lily, Lord. She needs you now. Surround her with your divine protection."*

He hadn't exactly told Adora the truth when he said

he thought he knew where to look for Lily. He had a gut feeling, and if he was right, was she was likely in the direct path of the intruders.

He couldn't think about the possible repercussions. He had to stay calm and in control of his actions. Dispassionate.

He chuckled coldly. He knew he was beyond that now. He'd already done everything he'd been solemnly taught not to do.

He cared about the people he was protecting.

He gritted his teeth as he reached the veranda doors, which were closed but not locked. He looked carefully at the lock and door frame but could find no evidence of forced entry. He knew he ought to sweep the room, but instead, working on instinct alone, he slipped outside and stealthily made his way to the garden.

He was not running now, though everything inside him screamed to do so. But if Lily was indeed in trouble, he could not afford to give himself away.

He had to be slow. And careful.

He only hoped he was not too late.

Lily had found herself once again strolling through the garden late at night. It was a habit she was beginning to enjoy. The air was crisp and the flowers pungent, but what she found to be the best benefit by far was the utter silence of the night.

With the sky full of bright, twinkling stars in a cloudless night, it was easy to see the path before her, the benches marking points to rest and admire the gardener's lovely handiwork, and the large white gazebo in the middle of the garden, looking gray and shadowy in the moonlight.

She felt a slight chill and rubbed her hands against the gooseflesh on her arms. She really should have brought a jacket, she reprimanded herself firmly.

At least the cold took her mind off her real dilemma—Kevin MacCormack. In truth she'd come out here to try to unscramble her mixed-up feelings about the man.

She felt foolish and awkward, like a teenager in the worst stages of a crush.

But maybe that was just it.

She was *feeling* again.

She thought her heart had died when she'd buried David, that she had experienced her only turn at love in the world, and now it was gone.

But the past few days, emotions she'd thought never to feel again had washed over her, making her laugh and cry at the oddest moments. And it was glorious.

No matter how hard she tried, she couldn't keep her eyes off Kevin. Whenever their gazes met, her heart raced. And when he was not there, the house felt strangely empty.

He had done so much for her family, for her little girl, that she could never repay him. But he was the type of man who didn't look for payment—not earthly payment, anyway. She had heard him tell Abigail about how good deeds were treasured up in heaven where they could never be stolen or taken away.

He must have an acre of gold, piled higher than a person could see, for all the good deeds he had done. A smile drifted to her face just thinking about it.

He was the most wonderful and unique man she had ever met. And though her first love, David, would always have a special place in her heart, she suddenly realized she had the capability to love again.

Maybe it was because Kevin and David were as different as night from day. She was falling in love with a *nurse.* How ironic was that?

She had just realized she no longer felt cold when she heard a movement in the bushes behind her. Thinking it was a squirrel or raccoon, she whirled around, intending to shoo it away.

What she met instead was a giant of a man, burly and brusque, with a baseball cap pulled low over his brow and a red bandanna tucked over his chin.

Despite the ball cap, she could see his eyes, small, black, cold and beady. She immediately opened her mouth to scream.

Before she could utter a single syllable, the stranger had her around the waist, his dirty hand clapped over her mouth. She struggled in his grasp, but there was no contest for strength.

All she could think of was Abigail.

It must be the reason this man was here. She now realized her mistake in not telling her mother or one of the servants where she had gone. No one knew she was out here in the darkened garden with a criminal's hand slapped over her face.

Think, Lily, she urged herself.

She had taken self-defense classes just after David had died, but the moves eluded her frantic mind. She could hear the sound of her own heartbeat rushing in her ears, and had the sudden fear she might pass out.

That did it.

She straightened in the man's arms as much as she could, given the circumstances, and pushed her chin up with all her might.

Lily Montague was not the passing-out type. She would face these circumstances with every bit of dignity she could muster. Her mother might even be proud.

Just then she heard another rustle from the bushes across from her and another man appeared. Like the first man, he looked every bit the thug, with his hat and his scarf and his unshaven cheeks, but this man was tall and lanky, and there was intelligence brimming in his eyes.

Lily stopped fighting in the burly man's arms and tried to think. Her adrenaline was surging and panic screamed in her ears.

She had to keep Abigail safe; these must be the men she'd feared would come.

She looked from one man to the other, once again sizing them up. It would be worthless, she realized, to try to reason with them—as if she could, with one of the thug's big, grimy paws slapped across her mouth.

Some of her self-defense moves were coming back to her, but what good would they do now? She might have been able to take on one man, but surely not two.

Especially two men with guns.

But she would not give in, not with as much as was at stake. She would protect her daughter at all costs, even with her own life if need be.

Breathing in through her nose and barely overcoming the instinctive urge to gag, she abruptly shifted and jammed her heel into the thug's instep, while at the same time biting his hand as hard as she could.

The big lug howled in pain and fury, hopping on one leg and shaking his hand in the air. It was exactly the motion Lily was waiting for, and she immediately rolled out of his grasp.

He glared at her but didn't immediately rush after her to capture her again. Lily eyed him warily, but it was the other man, the tall, thin fellow, who worried her more at the moment.

He was chuckling darkly, his sharp blue eyes gleaming with amusement as he pointed his weapon directly at her head. "Nice move, Ms. Montague. Not too many people get away from my brawny associate here." The thin one tipped his cap at her. "Like I said—*ni-i-ice.*"

The way he said it sent shivers down her spine. Lily had frozen from the moment her name was mentioned, not that she could have gone anywhere with a gun pointed at her head. But any remaining hope that these two ruffians were common thieves was detonated by the familiar way he used her name.

"What do you want?" she demanded sharply, happy her voice wasn't shaking the way she was quivering on the inside.

"Like you don't know," spat the burly one, cradling his wounded hand to his chest and continuing to glare at her vehemently. His voice held a bit of a Southern accent, Lily noted, while the other man sounded well-educated and his voice did not contain an accent which she could perceive.

Deciding to ignore the big, ornery thug who was still hopping around and calling her bad names, she turned her attention to the tall, thin fellow, who was, after all, still pointing a loaded gun at her head.

He appeared to be the brains of the operation. There was a small chance she could reason with him.

He was smirking at his partner's antics, but one eye was always on her. "Don't play around with us, missy. We don't want to hurt you, so just be calm and cooperate with us."

"I'll never cooperate with you," she said boldly, lifting her chin.

"Oh, yes you will. We want to see your girl. Now lead us to her."

Lily's worst fears were coming true, and there was no doubt he noticed her reaction, for his smile grew wide and his eyes gleamed.

"Why don't you make it easy on yourself and your little girl and lead the way?" he said in a soft and terrifyingly cajoling manner.

She straightened and looked down the barrel of the gun and into his eyes. "She's not here."

"Liar!" the large man cried. For as big as he was, he moved with lightning swiftness, bunching his thick arms around Lily before she knew what he wanted to do.

This time he braced his feet apart and out of reach of her sharp heels. And he didn't try to gag her with his hand, either.

Instead, he put his gun to her head, which was much more effective. Lily froze, feeling as if her heart wasn't even beating.

"No more words," he growled ferociously. "Where's the girl?"

"I told you she's not here," Lily replied with as much force as she could.

The man squeezed her ribs until she cried out. "Don't mess with us, lady. We ain't gonna hurt your kid. We just wanna talk to her for a little bit. That ain't so bad, now, is it?"

Lily tilted her chin and remained silent. The man squeezed her ribs again and she gritted her teeth, refusing to give him the pleasure of hearing her groan or scream in pain.

Surely they had to know she would die before giving her darling Abigail into their filthy hands. She closed her eyes, earnestly praying but knowing help would not come.

"Gentlemen, I don't think it will be necessary for you to see Abigail this evening."

The sound of Kevin's welcome deep bass voice was almost too much for Lily to bear. Her heart sang with elation.

She twisted in her captive's arms so she could see where Kevin was standing. He might be a nurse, but he was a big, muscular man. At least it would be two on two, and it hadn't sounded as if he was playing around when he addressed the two thugs.

Even so, she wasn't prepared for what she saw when she turned around.

Kevin wasn't dressed in scrubs or even sweats. He wore black jeans and a close-fitting, shadowy black T-shirt complemented by a black belt and black sneakers. He looked as if he'd been prepared to sneak around in the dark this time.

And he had a gun pointed directly at her.

The jolt of surprise almost physically hurt. Not only did Kevin have a gun, he had a shoulder holster strapped around him.

Lily shivered.

What kind of a nurse carried a gun?

The only people she knew who carried their sidearms in shoulder holsters were detectives, FBI and maybe some higher-level criminals.

All of these impressions flew through her mind at lightning speed as Kevin stepped forward into the moonlight, his face grim and his gun still pointed directly at her head. He was watching the two men and didn't make eye contact with her.

It didn't take a genius to see he knew how to use the pistol in his hand. Her heart sank into her toes as she realized Kevin must have betrayed her, infiltrated their family and earned their trust so he could take Abigail away.

Fury raged through her as she glared at Kevin. She had *trusted* him. She wanted to scream and cry and throw herself at him, but even if the burly thug's thick arms weren't clamped around her, she doubted she would have been able to move. She felt incredibly heavy, as if she had lead running through her veins and concrete bricks on her feet.

How could he have done this to her? To Abigail? How could she have been so wrong about his character?

She had actually thought he might be growing to care for her, and certainly for sweet little Abigail. It had been so obvious. Maybe too obvious, in retrospect.

"Hello, Mack," the big thug said gruffly from behind her ear. His breath stank of liquor, and Lily stiffened in distaste.

Who was Mack?

She looked around for a third man, but the only one there was Kevin. She experienced another jolt of bitter understanding when it became obvious what was going on.

Kevin wasn't even Kevin. His real name was Mack, or at least that was what he was called, as she realized "Mack" was a nickname based on his last name.

He obviously knew these men, and they knew him. He was in league with them.

His next words confirmed her worst fears.

"Donnelly," Mack responded, his gaze taking in every nuance of the situation. He held his bold position, his voice warm and even. He hoped Lily would feel at least a measure of comfort from his presence, from the confidence in his voice. She had to know he would rescue her, even if she thought he was only a nurse.

He was relieved when Donnelly took his gun from Lily's temple and aimed it at him. That was exactly what he wanted to happen.

Lily made a surprised sound, her eyes wide as she looked at Donnelly's revolver. She looked back at Kevin, her gaze hazy and confused.

Poor Lily.

This was surely the worst situation she'd ever experienced, and he knew she had to be terrified. He tried to reassure her with his gaze, and was happy to see a measure of calm return to her bright eyes.

"What are you doing here, Mack?" the other man asked, sounding surly about the prospect.

As well he should, Mack thought grimly.

"Well, Finch, I was out taking a late-night stroll when I heard a noise." He knew he wasn't answering the question the man was asking, but he was being purposefully vague. "Now, what would you two lugheads be doing out and about at this time of night? You're up to no good, I'm thinking. Do you want me to take you in to the bureau, so you can explain this little shenanigan?"

"Put your gun down, Mack," Finch said, his voice a command clearly expected to be obeyed. "You're outnumbered and outgunned."

Mack lifted his eyebrows. "Am I?"

Shifting subtly, he made eye contact with Lily. She looked frightened, but not panicked.

Good. That was what he needed. It was imperative Lily keep a cool head on her shoulders right now. And he prayed with all his heart she would understand the message he communicated in his gaze, for if she did not, taking the two men down would be much more difficult.

He needed her help.

He breathed a sigh of relief at the infinitesimal nod of her head. He had always thought they had a strange sort of inward connection between them, and he blessed the Lord for that now.

"I'll shoot you if I have to," Finch warned, waving his gun in a threatening manner.

"Not if I kill you first." Mack's gun was steadily pointed, and he didn't move a muscle. Lily's life depended on his aim. He was a sharpshooter and confident in his abilities. It was just the sight of Lily helpless in Donnelly's grasp that made his stomach drop.

He slid a glance at Finch, who was slowly nudging his way toward Donnelly.

Good. That would make what he had to do easier. He stood and waited until the men were about two feet apart, and then inwardly tensed for action.

"So, Finch, who hired you?" He knew the question would throw the man off guard, and Finch began stammering and stuttering.

"Now, Lily," he called, hoping beyond hope she had read his signals right.

He had a backup plan, but Lily's life was at stake, and he didn't want to make it any more difficult on her than it already was. He prayed he wouldn't have to use his backup.

Lily screamed and blasted her elbow into Donnelly's rib cage. He howled and apparently loosened his grip, for Lily hit the ground in a second.

Exactly what Mack had wanted.

Mack fired off two rounds—one into Donnelly's shoulder and the other into Finch's thigh. He dove forward and tackled Finch to the ground, rolling him and cuffing his hands behind his back in a matter of seconds.

Only then could he take the time to see how Lily was faring.

Donnelly was bigger and a great deal heavier than

Lily. Even with a bullet in his shoulder, it was conceivable he could take her down.

He held his breath as he turned to look. The sight he found took the breath from his lungs in a rush.

Chapter Seven

Lily was on her feet as fast as she'd dropped to the ground. Big, burly Donnelly was howling in pain, his gun covering the wound in his thick shoulder.

She didn't have time to feel nauseated. She didn't feel anything at all.

She simply reacted.

Rushing at the big man, she grabbed his gun with both hands and pushed and twisted it away from him so he had no choice but to drop it onto the walk.

Lily scrambled to pick it up. The harsh steel felt cold and awkward in her hands.

At first, she balanced the gun and aimed it at Donnelly, but a glance at a stunned-looking Kevin, who was kneeling on an already downed and cuffed Finch, made her realize how ridiculous she must look.

She'd never fired a gun in her life, and she wasn't about to start now.

With a loud huff of breath, she tossed the revolver into a nearby bush and once again rushed Donnelly. He was still howling, and he scrambled backward when Lily let out a banshee yell.

He was bigger and weighed at least a hundred pounds more than she did, but he was acting like a wounded animal, and Lily knew she had to use that to her advantage.

But wounded animals were dangerous, and she was on her guard.

She gritted her teeth and pushed one palm into his wound as hard as she could, while using her other hand to lever his arm up. Every ounce of her strength was caught up in the motion, and she found she was still yelling like a wildcat.

As she'd hoped, Donnelly dropped to the ground from the pressure she had put upon him. She jumped on him, nailing her knee to his chest as hard as she could and keeping his bad arm twisted in the air.

She might be able to keep the man down for a moment or two, but not much more. What was she supposed to do now? It wasn't as if she had been trained for such things, and unlike Kevin, she didn't have a pair of handcuffs to slap on the man.

She slid a quick glance at Kevin to plead for his help, but dropped Donnelly's arm in surprise at what she saw.

Kevin was surrounded by FBI agents, all with their guns drawn. She didn't need to be kneeling on Donnelly, either, she realized. Agents were even now surrounding them with their guns drawn, taking the responsibility for the criminals.

With things obviously well in hand, Kevin had holstered his gun and was approaching her quickly, concern lining his face. He looked big, hardened and completely in control. Lily didn't know what to make of it.

Grasping her hands, he lifted her gently off the bulky criminal and led her by the shoulders to the nearest bench. He urged her to sit down in the same rich, gentle voice she had always known.

She was shaking now, in the aftermath of panic. She clenched her hands in her lap, lacing her fingers together in a nervous gesture to keep her tremor from being too obvious.

Kevin obviously noticed, for he placed his big, warm hand over hers and squeezed reassuringly. "Take slow, deep breaths," he coached softly. "Try to think of something else, Lily."

She glanced at him. He was watching her with concerned, kind eyes. She tipped him a shaky smile to let him know all was well.

"Shouldn't you be out helping those fellows?" she asked, remembering suddenly that this wasn't Kevin, her daughter's sweet, kind nurse, but someone called Mack, who was apparently connected to the FBI in some way—some way she didn't want to know.

She looked away, unable to meet his gaze any longer, knowing her eyes would give her away.

"They've got it handled," he said shortly. "Donnelly and Finch are just a couple of hired guns for whoever kidnapped Jeremy."

He paused. "You know, you were great out there. A guy would never know it was your first time facing down bad guys. Maybe *you* should have been the one to consider a career with the FBI."

She turned with such velocity she nearly gave herself whiplash. His eyes were shining with tenderness and mirth, at least until he saw the expression on her face. Then his smile melted to a stiff frown and his dark eyebrows knitted together in a straight, low line.

She looked away.

"I was only kidding, you know," he said, clearing his throat. "I didn't mean anything by it."

"Of course you were," she said dryly. "A career in the FBI is more your style, isn't it, Kevin? Or should I call you Mack?"

His jaw dropped and he stared at her, astonished and clearly guilty as charged. He didn't have to speak to confirm it.

"So, who hired you, then? My mother?"

He gave a clipped nod.

"I figured."

Oh, yes. It was all coming together very clearly now. Lily wouldn't accept FBI support, so Adora, acting in what she thought was her granddaughter's best interest, went behind Lily's back and brought the FBI into her house without her knowledge.

Which meant Kevin was much more than a nurse, if he was a nurse at all, which she was beginning to doubt.

There were so many ramifications to this revelation. Kevin must have been nearby even when she'd thought him off duty.

She felt sick, as much from Kevin's exposure as from the terrible situation she had just experienced. The big thug had pointed a loaded gun at her head. Now she felt Kevin was the one aiming the gun at her temple. Her head was whirling with the assimilation of facts she had just discovered and the many complicated questions the gaps proposed.

"I don't believe this," she said at last, turning on the one person she could lash out at in all this. "I trusted you, Kevin. I believed everything you said to me. And you betrayed me."

"Lily, I—" he began, but she immediately cut him off.

"Save it for someone who cares," she quipped bitterly, turning her back on him.

She didn't want to hear his side of the story. Not now, at least.

He growled in frustration and stood, moving to help out the men with the crime scene.

Lily watched him walk away, her teeth clenched as tightly as her hands. Everyone in her life except her daughter had conspired against her.

Who knew? Maybe even Abigail knew she was under Kevin's protection.

Was Lily the only one in the dark?

She wouldn't be surprised by anything at this point. This night had been the grand finale of her life, as far as she was concerned. Her whole world was being rocked as if she'd been hit by the biggest bolt of lightning ever known. Even her skin was buzzing with the electricity.

She had held off an intruder—a criminal with a loaded pistol! She never knew she had it in her. For some reason, she'd always thought she would faint if something awful like this happened to her.

But she hadn't.

She'd stood on her own two feet and done what needed to be done, even if she was too shaken to stand up now that the deed was done.

She had saved her daughter.

Kevin had saved Abigail.

Whatever Lily had done, it would not have been enough had Kevin not shown up when he had. He had saved her, as well as Abigail. Who knew what the two thugs were really up to? They said they only wanted to talk, but she knew they would have taken off with Abigail, and they could have killed her.

The world was so full of hate and violence. Lily had never worn rose-colored glasses, and she thought she knew how it was. Her husband had been killed by the evil workings of criminals.

And still violence dogged her, no matter where she hid.

Now, at least, two bad men were going to jail, and Kevin was carrying a sidearm—openly, she supposed. He'd probably had a gun all along.

Her mind drifted back to the day of the indoor picnic, when he'd backed off so suddenly. She'd never quite gotten over that rejection, but she realized now he couldn't allow her to touch him. He had a gun strapped to his chest and she would have discovered his secret.

No wonder he'd scrambled away. And how he had hurt her tentative feelings for him with that action. It seemed so silly now she almost wanted to laugh.

What a fool she'd been. Couldn't she have put all the puzzle pieces together and come up with a coherent explanation for the things around her before now?

And if she hadn't known Kevin was FBI when he was living in her own—well, her mother's—house, how would she be able to recognize any kind of real threat to her daughter?

Kevin walked toward her, his hands outstretched and a half smile on his face.

She glared at him, but accepted his help to stand. He didn't immediately let her go, his thumbs gently stroking her palms.

"Do you have your sea legs yet?" he asked in a teasing voice, though the humor he conveyed in his voice for once didn't reach his green eyes, which had lost their customary glittering sparkle.

She pulled her hands away as soon as she was certain she wouldn't fall on her behind and humiliate herself even more than she already had.

"I only want to know one thing," she said, her throat closing around her words and making her voice high and squeaky.

He looked for a moment as if he thought she were about to smack him in the face, but then a determined look took over as he squared his shoulders and clenched his jaw. "What? I'll tell you anything you want to know, if I am able."

She seethed inside at the typical FBI reply. As if she was going to ask some kind of state secret or something. Her ire grew with every moment she stayed in his presence.

"You can relax. I'm not going to ask for the keys to the White House."

He barked out a crisp chuckle.

"I have a more pertinent question." She paused, letting him sweat a little bit. When he looked as of he was in complete agony, she continued. "Is your name Kevin, or is it Mack?"

He cleared his throat, looking this way and that to avoid her gaze.

She waited patiently, knowing eventually he would have to look at her. And answer the question.

When she met his green-eyed gaze, she felt a moment of remorse, but then quickly reminded herself *she* was the wounded one here. She stood an inch taller and crossed her arms. "Well?"

"Well…" he hedged for a moment, and then finally met her gaze. "Honestly? Both."

"Honestly?" she echoed, her gaze boring into his. At least he had the decency to flinch.

She shook her head and turned away from him, walking as quickly as she could without looking as if she was running away.

"Lily," Kevin called after her, running to catch up. "Can I say something?"

She stopped so suddenly he ran into her back, then had to grasp her around the hips to keep her from taking a dive onto the concrete.

She turned in his arms, as it quickly became apparent he wasn't going to let her go. He stared down at her, his face a maze of emotion. Lily's lungs stopped working completely, leaving her breathless and dizzy. It was the aftermath of the crisis, and not his embrace, which was causing all this havoc, she convinced herself.

"Make it fast," she squeaked, wishing the bitterness she was feeling in her heart could in some way make it to her voice. But she was surprised she could speak at all, as ravaged as she was feeling.

He bent his head down close to hers so their eyes could meet, and his breath was warm and soothing against her cheek.

Still, he didn't speak, but just stood holding her and gazing into her eyes.

And she had never been more uncomfortable in her life. She wished he would let her go, but she knew she had no more strength to fight him. She thought he knew it, as well.

She fought as much as she could. She held her hands stiffly at her sides and kept her chin tilted toward the night sky.

She had been betrayed by this man. She would not now offer him the olive branch he obviously desired.

He had been lying to her since the moment he walked in through the door of her mother's house. The laughter, the emotional connection she felt with him—it was all a ruse. She had been completely taken in by his roguish charm, and now she would pay very dearly for her mistake, though at the moment she felt oddly numb, even reassured by his strong arms wrapped so tenderly about her.

"I know you think I'm a liar," he said, low and gruff in her ear. "I know how bad this looks from your perspective. You think I deceived you."

"Didn't you?" she snapped back.

"Yes. And it was a willful deception, made with my full knowledge and consent. But I was never comfortable with it."

"Then why did you do it?" she snapped, bitterness now lining her voice.

"Because of Abigail."

His words pierced into her heart, especially when he

didn't continue right away. When he did, it was only to drive the dagger more deeply into her wound and turning it for good measure.

"You refused FBI help. Your mother didn't. I've worked undercover before, Lily, but I've never had a reason to question what I was doing. I wanted—needed—to take care of sweet little Abigail."

He paused and pulled in a deep breath. "And I wanted to look after you. But you know as well as I do you would not have accepted my protection if I had freely offered it."

That much was true, Lily had to admit. And in the end, he had been right.

He had saved Abigail. And he'd saved her, too, for she never would have been able to fight those two thugs on her own.

"I'm sure it's not the first time you've been undercover," she said thoughtfully as she reconsidered everything he had told her. "What made this particular mission so much of a problem for you?"

"You."

She leaned back. "Me? What did I have to do with anything, except having to make your whole operation hush-hush?"

"You touched my heart." He took one hand from her waist and took her hand, placing her palm on his chest. Over his heart. "You made me care."

His voice got husky. "I'm not supposed to care, Lily. Not on the job."

"I don't want to hear this, Kevin. Or Mack. Or whoever you are." She tilted her chin up and reined in her emotions as much as possible.

"Well, you're going to, sweetheart, because I'm not letting you go until I'm finished talking."

His pet name left her heart whirling as fast as her head was. "Then talk."

"I want you to know something, and I give my word that it is the truth. What we had building between us—what we shared—that was real."

"I have no idea what you're talking about," she snapped with a futile attempt to look anywhere except at Kevin.

"Now who is lying?"

She tried to pull away again, but his arm was tight around her waist.

"I care for you, Lily. A lot. And I hope someday soon we can build a bridge between us, or at least begin again as friends."

Except he'd forgotten one crucial thing.

There would be no tomorrow. He'd done his work, and now he would be leaving. Those two men in custody would squeal on Jeremy's kidnapper in short order.

He leaned down as if to kiss her, but she turned her head so his lips brushed lightly against her cheek. She was going to cry if she stayed here, and the one thing she could not do was cry in front of Kevin ever again.

"Goodbye," she choked out, then turned and broke away from his grasp.

"See you later, Lily," he called after her, though he didn't try to follow.

Yeah, right. She'd heard those words before.

From David. Right before he was killed.

Later that night, Mack escorted Adora back to her bedroom, assuring her all was safe for the night, and then tucked Abby into bed and read her a bedtime story until she dropped off to sleep. No one had seen Lily since she left the garden.

It wasn't until he'd settled himself into his small room for the night that he saw Lily, from the two-way mirror, sneak into Abby's room and kneel before her daughter's bedside.

It was the first time all night he had seen tears in her eyes, though she had been through such a horrible, frightening ordeal he thought she would have been crying long ago.

She was the strongest woman he'd ever known.

She was young, yet she'd already been through a lifetime full of pain and grief. He admired her spirit— and he admired even more the woman kneeling even now by her child's bedside.

Was she in prayer? He hoped she'd found a little strength and peace in God over the month since he'd been here. He knew she was fiercely independent. God would not be the first place she would turn in trouble. But he hoped maybe now, in a time of crisis, she might reach for the God who was already reaching for her.

Mack watched as she crawled gently into bed with the little girl and wrapped Abby in her arms. He wished he could slide through the mirror door and join them, wrap his arms around both of them and assure them of their safety and his affection.

But he couldn't assure them of safety, especially now that the house had been breached, and Lily certainly didn't want anything to do with his affection.

So instead, he propped himself up on his cot, leaned his back against the wall and watched them until he fell into an uneasy sleep.

When he awoke early the next morning, he was surprised to find Lily was still in bed with Abby. She must have dozed off there, finding comfort in keeping the daughter she had almost lost more than once tucked safely in her arms.

Mack showered, shaved and then paused, wondering what to wear. There was no ruse anymore, yet Abby might be more comfortable if he wore scrubs.

In the end, he pulled on a pair of black jeans and a black T-shirt, his usual fare. And he wore his gun on the outside, where everyone could see it plainly. Abby had been told he carried a gun. Lily was going to have to come to terms with him eventually.

He was what he was, a government special agent, and

he decided he might as well not tiptoe around the issue anymore.

He was seated at the breakfast table eating a banana when Lily came into the kitchen. He almost laughed at the way her eyes widened and her jaw gaped to see him there at the table, and even more when her gaze shifted to the gun at his shoulder.

She quickly recovered, however, and reached for an orange from the fruit basket, taking the seat across from him and peeling the fruit slowly and methodically, with each piece of skin the same size and shape. It was so typically Lily.

She didn't look at him, but he knew she was keenly aware of him. And her hands were shaking just the tiniest bit, giving her calm, composed facade away.

"Surprised to see me?" he quipped, reaching for another banana.

Her head popped up and their gazes met and locked. "Yes."

"My mission is not over, you know. We caught a couple of henchmen, but we haven't nabbed the bad guy yet. And until that happens, Abby is in danger."

"Abigail," Lily snapped. "Her name is Abigail."

Mack quirked an apologetic smile, since he had been calling the little girl Abby since the day he'd first come to the mansion. "Yeah, right. Sorry."

"So what's your point?" she asked. "I assume you have one."

"Oh, I do," he assured her. "I have much more than a point. I have a plan."

"Point, plan, whatever," she muttered under her breath, then slowly bit into her orange.

"Lily, it's not safe for Abby—*Abigail* to stay here anymore," he said gently.

She looked at the table. "I knew you were going to say that."

"Then we agree," he said more cheerfully than he felt. He hadn't thought she would have given in so easily, and his heart was soaring. She must still trust him a little bit, right? "We need to take her somewhere else, somewhere she will be truly safe," he continued, putting one hand behind his neck and stretching back in his chair.

"I didn't *agree* to anything," she said, shaking her head. "Not yet. Where, exactly, do you think you could take her where she would be safe?"

"Listen to the man," Adora said with a big yawn, scuffing into the kitchen in a plush bathrobe and fuzzy pink slippers that suited her to perfection, her hair still in curlers.

Mack nearly slid out of his seat. Never had Adora been seen at anything less than her best, and he had no notion why she'd picked today to change her habits, unless it was to annoy her daughter.

It was amusing him.

"I'm listening, mother," Lily said through gritted teeth. "Why don't both of you try and tell me what's going on here? You obviously have some reason you're up before noon."

Mack had to clamp his lips shut to keep from bellowing with laughter. It was a serious day and a likewise serious matter, but Lily hadn't mentioned a word about her mother's bathrobe or pink, fuzzy slippers.

"Colorado," he said when he could speak without fear of breaking into laughter. "The Rocky Mountains, to be precise."

Lily's gaze shifted to him. "Why?"

"Because it's far, far away from the bad guys and what happened last night," he said, his voice sobering. "And for another thing, a change of scenery might help Abby—er—Abigail to heal faster."

"Go on," she said, her voice even but with more than a hint of suspicion.

"Look, Lily," he said, leaning forward. "We can get her better care up there, have more staff to help her. A physical therapist. And a child psychologist to help her work through her issues."

"Abigail already has a shrink, as you well know," she insisted, leaning back in her chair and crossing her arms. She glared at him as if he was a rattlesnake.

"It'd be a new start," he insisted.

"Listen to the man," Adora repeated.

"Please, Mom. Don't you think you've done enough already?" Lily pleaded.

Adora huffed and moved toward the coffeepot. "If

you had any sense, I wouldn't have had to do anything, young lady."

Oh, boy. Mack braced for the explosion, but there was none.

Lily's shoulders slumped. "You're right. Go on, Kevin. Or do you want me to call you Mack?" she said, with a moment's hesitation.

"Kevin is fine," he said, and realized it was. Lily was the only one in the world who called him by his given name, and that made it special.

"A psychologist might be able to help Abby talk about what happened," he said, folding his hands onto the table in front of him. "And that is very important, Lily. There is a little boy out there who isn't safe, who doesn't have his mother to protect him."

Lily clapped a hand over her mouth and tears rushed to her eyes. "I'd almost forgotten," she admitted. "I was so caught up with Abigail, that I—"

"Of course you were," he said, bursting in before she could lay more guilt upon her shoulders. "All your attention was and should be on Abby. But in addition to protecting Abby, I've also got a duty to that little boy. If Abby can help us find out where he is—"

"Okay," she agreed with sudden ardor. "Just tell me what to do to get ready. We'll go wherever you want us to go. Just find that boy."

Adora walked across the room with her coffee. Mack thought she was going to sit down at the table, but instead, the older woman went to stand behind her daughter, and placed one hand on her shoulder with a gentle, supportive squeeze.

It might not have seemed like much to the casual onlooker, but Mack knew what it meant to Lily.

Tears slid silently down her cheeks.

Chapter Eight

It amazed Lily how quickly Kevin made a simple discussion over the breakfast table into reality.

They were on a private jet to Colorado by mid-afternoon and settled into their quiet cabin tucked into Rocky Mountain National Park near the town of Estes Park before the sun had time to set over the snow-tipped mountain peaks.

Lily's head was awhirl. Too much information and too much activity. FBI men were all about, securing the area and making sure the cabin was comfortable. Someone made a roaring fire in the fireplace, and the enticing smell of chili simmered on the stove.

Kevin had fawned over Abigail all day, making sure she was comfortable during the trip and that she lacked for nothing. He even spoiled her with an extra soda, once he got permission from Lily.

But even though Kevin's attention was caught up with her daughter, he was not too busy to forget about Lily. When she was ushered from place to place, it was always Kevin's big, gentle hand on her arm guiding her.

In fact, it seemed to be an unspoken rule among the agents that Lily was Kevin's territory, for few of the men spoke to her or interacted with her, and then only in Kevin's presence.

She didn't know how she felt about that. Everything was new and rushed.

And *changed*.

Especially where Kevin was concerned.

He was the same tender, considerate man he had always been, with his big green eyes streaming affection and compassion every time he looked at her. And yet, he was none of the things Lily thought he was. He was a fantasy she'd created in her mind, and the truth hurt.

"Are you even a nurse?" she asked him when they had both settled back on the couch to eat the steaming chili and share a hot loaf of sourdough bread.

She knew there were other agents on the premises, circling the house and keeping lookout for any kind of danger, but Kevin was the only agent placed inside the cabin with her and Abigail. And she was certain that was no accident. Actually, if she was honest with herself, she was glad. At least she knew him. A little.

Kevin chuckled and shook his head. "I was wondering when you were going to get around to asking me that question."

He took a tentative sip of chili off his spoon, then jerked back as the sauce evidently burned his lips. His spoon clattered into the bowl as he reached for his napkin with one hand and a cold glass of water with the other.

Lily couldn't help but laugh. She tore a piece of bread from the loaf and handed it to him. "Try this. It'll work better than water to put out that fire on your tongue."

He gave her a panicked, wide-eyed look and quickly took a large bite of bread, chewing slowly as his expression returned to normal. "How did you know to do that?"

Lily shrugged. "A lot of dishes in the South are hot— either temperature-wise or spicy. I think my mother must have taught me that bread trick. I was always getting into things as a child, including food at fancy parties. I think I nearly burned my tongue off with some Cajun gumbo I tried once."

He laughed. "I'm a meat-and-potatoes man, myself. Stick to the basics, don't feed me anything green, and we're set."

She was about to say she'd already guessed he was probably a meat-and-potatoes kind of guy, but she kept the comment for later as another, more serious thought passed through her mind.

"I am really worried about my mother. She's all alone at that mansion now, and the bad guys know right where that is. What if they come back?"

"I didn't think you two were close," he said in surprise. "Weren't you the one who told me you took off running the moment you turned eighteen and didn't look back?" he teased lightly.

"Well, maybe I can chalk that up to being young and stupid."

"And your mother being, oh, shall we say a *little* controlling?"

Despite herself, Lily laughed and swatted Kevin's arm. "So you've noticed, have you?"

He chuckled. "How could I not? Your mother is a wonderful woman in her own way, but she does like to have things just the way she wants them. I'm not surprised a teenaged Lily went out of her mind and made a break for it."

"Don't tease me."

"I'm not. I assure you, I'm perfectly serious." He made a halfhearted attempt to straighten his mouth from the broad smile he wore, but was completely unsuccessful in his efforts.

"Do you think my mom is going to be all right?" Lily asked again. She had begged her mother to accompany them to Colorado, but Adora would hear nothing of it.

She would just be in the way of what needed doing, she told them bluntly. Besides, it was her house, and there wasn't any number of bad guys who could chase her out of it.

No, she would keep living just as she had been, and

Kevin and Lily would take good care of her grand-daughter in Colorado. It was her last word on the matter, and no amount of persuasion could talk her out of it.

"Adora doesn't know it, but I set an extra two men on her house. Trust me, she won't be bothered by any more thugs. Besides, I'm sure it's been through the criminal grapevine now that Abby has flown the coop. They have no reason to go to the house."

"Those guys can't follow us, can they?"

Kevin shook his head. "No way. If you believe nothing else about me, Lily, you can trust my sincerity. I'm good at my job."

Despite everything they'd been through, or maybe because of it, she believed him completely. She had already proved it. She was trusting him with Abigail's life, as well as her own.

"Which brings me back to my original question."

"Am I a nurse," Kevin said bluntly. "I haven't forgotten you'd asked." He paused and grinned. "What do you think?"

"I think I should have figured out you were a special agent a lot earlier than I did. I think you're a big, tough, gun-toting brute of a man."

He laughed. "I am that," he said. "But I'm also a registered nurse, compliments of the army. So you don't have to worry on that score. I always have and will continue to take good physical care of Abby."

She started to correct him on her child's name, but

then, for reasons she couldn't explain even to herself, she closed her mouth and remained silent.

Kevin took a tentative bite of the now-cooled chili, and they both ate in silence, each lost in their own thoughts.

Odd, but it wasn't an uncomfortable silence for Lily. That they could sit together and not talk was amazing—it spoke volumes of their true relationship, the one they never talked about.

After dinner, Kevin took up the dishes to wash, and Lily checked on Abigail, who was sleeping soundly in her large, new log bed, with fluffy comforters tucked up around her ears. Lily could barely see her daughter, but was reassured by the evenness of her breathing.

When she returned to the small main room of the cabin, Kevin had kicked off his boots and was stretched out on the rug in front of the fireplace, his chin cupped in his hand. He didn't turn when she came in, so she stood silently watching him for a moment.

He looked lost in thought, staring into the fire. His face had lost all its tenseness, and he appeared to be at peace. A small smile hovered on his lips.

"What's got you smiling?" she asked, moving around the sofa to sit cross-legged in front of him on the floor.

"I was praying," he admitted.

"Must have been a great prayer."

"Not a great prayer—a great God. Do you realize how much He has done for us? Even pulling Donnelly and Finch down was a major miracle."

"But you looked so calm when you confronted them. I was sure you could easily have taken them both with no trouble."

He belted out a laugh. "I'm good at bluffing. I would consider either one of those men an even match for me, but both together?"

He paused a moment. "I don't think so. They are highly trained, highly paid criminals, even if they look like bums."

"Wow," she said, her breath coming out in a gasp. "Then I could have been—"

She shivered. She was afraid to finish the sentence. She didn't want to think of what could have happened at all.

"But you weren't."

"Thanks to you," she said immediately.

He grinned. "Mostly thanks to God. I can't take the credit." He looked back into the fire for a moment, then turned his head to meet her gaze.

When he reached out for her, she tentatively placed her hand in his. "I don't want to think about what might have happened. I'm just glad you're safe."

"Me, too," she agreed, squeezing his hand. "I have to admit, I'm starting to relax out here in this cabin in the middle of nowhere. For once I don't feel there are bad guys right outside my door anymore."

"No bad guys," he said soberly, then grinned. "But you will find an FBI agent or two posted at every door, so be forewarned if you try to go out and take a walk in the woods. They have been instructed not to let you go *anywhere* alone."

She chuckled softly. "I can't believe that sounds like a reassuring statement. Six months ago I would have bolted if you said that."

He nodded, his eyes gleaming warm and joyful in the firelight.

"I suppose if I felt like going on a walk, I could ask you to go with me?"

He stared at her for the longest moment, not moving, maybe not even breathing. Lily knew she wasn't. Her lungs had stopped working the moment their eyes met.

Slowly, ever so slowly, he let go of her hand and reached up to caress her hair back from her face. Over and over he ran the pads of his thumb and fingertips across her cheek, tenderly exploring her jaw, her ear, her eyes, her lips.

She trembled as he leaned forward, tucking his hand behind her neck and drawing her closer to him, never taking his eyes off hers.

His lips hovered over hers until she could feel the warmth of his breath on her cheek, but still he did not finish the action.

Everything inside her was screaming for him to kiss her. She hadn't known this kind of torture could exist, but the half inch between their lips felt like miles, and she yearned to cross the chasm between them.

His eyes questioned hers. Did she want this moment to stop? Did she want him to pull away?

She knew he would stop if she asked him to. He was that kind of man—honest, loyal, honorable.

"Lily," he whispered, his voice a deep, guttural growl that said more than the words themselves. I—"

"Kiss me," she whispered, and when he did not move fast enough, she reached up to grasp the collar on his cotton dress shirt and pulled him down to close the gap between them.

His lips were warm and his touch gentle, and his kiss was everything Lily thought a kiss should be. She closed her eyes to savor the moment.

And then his lips were gone.

His touch was gone.

It took a moment for Lily to return to earth from the heavens Kevin had taken her to, but slowly, she opened her eyes, blinking at the firelight.

He was still there, staring at her with emotions on his face she dared not name. Her head was still spinning, and she felt rather odd—not exactly shy, but sweet and delicate all of a sudden.

Cherished. Yes, *cherished* was the word she was looking for.

She smiled softly.

He smiled, too, and it rocked her world.

And then, much too slowly for Lily's comfort, he once again leaned forward, once again brushed his lips lightly against her suddenly sensitive mouth, over and over again, this time deepening the kiss until her heart beat frantically.

"I'll keep you safe," he whispered over her lips. His already normally deep voice was thick and husky, almost more a demonstrative growl than mere words. "Abby, too. I promise."

She had never felt so secure, or so treasured. She had a hard time speaking the words she so wanted to say to him.

"I know."

Mack didn't sleep a wink that night, thinking about the special time before the roaring fire he'd shared with Lily. He knew now that this wasn't some passing fling, some crazy crush he had on his boss's daughter because he'd been alone too long.

He was fall-down, drag-out, nuts-out-of-his-mind in love with Lily Montague. He wanted to put a ring on her finger and adopt little Abby as his own.

And, he decided with a swiftness that punched the breath from his lungs, as soon as this case was wrapped up, he would do just that.

He thought Abby would be thrilled with the idea, since they had grown so close over the past six weeks. He loved the little girl with surprising intensity, and he was certain she loved him, too.

And after last night, he had little doubt of Lily's feelings for him. He'd seen her emotions in her big brown eyes, the reflection of the firelight confirming what he already knew in his heart.

Somehow, she'd found it in her heart to forgive him, to love him despite his faults.

God was indeed good.

Lily had never slept better in her life. She credited the clean mountain air, but deep down she knew the real reason she was able to sleep without waking once in a night terror the way she usually did.

Kevin.

Everyone else in the place called him Mack, but he'd been Kevin to her for so long she couldn't think of him any other way. She pulled her soft cotton comforter up to her chin and stared out the window, her mind easily drifting back to the time they'd shared last night in front of the warm, bright fireplace.

A smile drifted to her lips. She hadn't been that happy in a long, long time.

Maybe ever.

There was something so safe, so gentle, about Kevin, that it was still hard for her to think of him as a special agent. As much as she'd balked at the idea of a male nurse when he'd first walked in the door of the Montague mansion, she almost thought she ought to be relieved he'd turned out to be one of the tough guys.

Except she'd gotten used to the idea of male nurses,

realized they could be just as good, as kind, and as gentle as any woman ever could be.

And Kevin had such a deep, personal relationship with Abigail. Of course, Abigail had always looked upon Kevin as her protector, from the first day she had known him, and so he had turned out to be.

The only one who'd been surprised by that fact had been Lily.

Sighing, she rested her forehead on her knees. If only she could somehow hold on to last night, to the laughter, the romance, the promise in his eyes. She wanted to preserve the way she felt when she was held in the strength of his arms.

But with morning came reality, and reality had a bitter taste.

She couldn't be thinking about Kevin right now, and he sure couldn't afford to be thinking about her. Abigail wasn't the only one with her life at stake—there was that dear little boy, Jeremy McCain. There were still no ransom notes, nor a motive, but the FBI maintained it as a kidnapping.

And they were counting on Abigail.

Lily was as certain as Kevin that her daughter held vital information deep within her subconscious. Now that they were here in the safety of the mountains, she prayed Abigail would find peace.

Only then would she be able to confront her trauma and find a way to fight through it. Only then would she be able to talk about it, maybe give the FBI some of the clues they needed to rescue Jeremy.

But what would she do about Kevin?

She knew he wouldn't back off. Going on with their daily lives as if nothing had happened might be the sensible, rational thing to do. But she knew Kevin well enough by now to know he didn't always listen to reason where his heart was concerned.

His passion showed in everything he did, and she had no false hopes he would pretend nothing had happened between them and go on with his work here, putting what must be first in their lives in its proper place and ignoring the rest.

But she could.

And she would. Someone had to keep the arrow on the mark, and Lily knew in her heart it would have to be her. She had a sick, ugly feeling at the pit of her stomach at the thought of what she would be forced to do to keep things between her and Kevin under control, but she knew it must be done.

She knew she was right.

Maybe, in a different time and a different place, there might have been something for her and Kevin.

But not here, and not now.

She rolled out of bed and quickly dressed, determined to face Kevin as soon as possible, so he would have no doubt as to her feelings, nor the course they must both take for the sake of the children involved.

But when she entered the main cabin, it was more like a freeway than a hideaway, and Lily was immediately confused by the chaos. Big, bulky men were moving here and there, hauling large pieces of equipment Lily assumed had to do with Abigail's physical therapy and calling out cheerful insults at each other.

More to the point, at least to Lily—there were two women present—*young* women—and they both appeared to be hanging on Kevin's every word, not to mention his muscular arms.

A blonde and a brunette, she noticed with a pique she could not contain. Now all he needed was a redhead and he would be all set, she thought, knowing she was being surly and not caring.

Lily felt a tinge of what she refused to acknowledge as jealousy, and then pasted a smile on her face and approached Kevin and the two women. "What's with the traffic?" she asked a little too brightly. "I thought we were in hiding here."

The young blonde burst into high, tinkling laughter that instantly put Lily's teeth on edge.

"They're not all staying," she explained in the same high-pitched whine. "Only Sandra and I."

The brunette nodded her head at Lily. "I'm a child psychiatrist, Ms. Montague. I'm here to help Abby get better."

"It's Abigail," Lily corrected automatically through still-clenched teeth. At least Sandra had to be old enough to get certified. She turned her attention to the blonde. "And you are?"

The young woman tittered again and Lily tried not to cringe, though she couldn't help the sharp gaze she tossed in the foolish woman's direction. Was she going to have to endure *this* madness every day for the rest of the unseen future?

She slipped a quick, furtive glance at Kevin to see how he was taking all this nonsense, but of course he was grinning widely, looking eager and ready to take on the world.

He would.

"I'm Marcy," the younger woman said. "The physical therapist."

How many years did a person have to go to school for physical therapy? This girl looked as if she was still in high school.

She acted that way, too, in Lily's opinion.

She didn't care whether she was being fair. Seeing Kevin surrounded with doting women hanging all over him and looking at him as if he was a piece of meat did nothing for her attitude.

Or her ego.

She looked carefully at the two women, hoping her gaze suggested the sensibility and control she *wasn't* feeling at the moment. "Shouldn't you be directing these muscle-bound agents as to where you want your equipment?"

She made a broad gesture which encompassed the entire room, up to and including the heaving, sweating agents. And the front door, but that was beside the point.

"Oh, no," Marcy said, rubbing her palm in tiny circles against Kevin's arm. "Mack is in charge. I don't have to worry about a thing."

"I see," Lily said, raising an eyebrow at Kevin. "In charge of everything, are you?"

She made sure he didn't miss the covert glances she made to the ladies by his side.

His smile dipped and faltered, but he quickly recovered, pulling one corner of his mouth up in a half smile. His gaze was apologetic, and Lily wondered if he was feeling guiltier about Marcy's high-toned sassy words or her own presence. Surely it was not the company of the pretty young ladies.

"I'm just trying to help," he croaked.

"Of course you are."

And it didn't hurt that he was helping a couple of beautiful women, now did it? Lily reined her thoughts in, refusing to be shallow. She was better than that.

Besides, given the current state of things, she had no reason for jealousy. It was not as if Kevin owed her anything.

"So, Mr. Coordinator, tell me what can I do to help out around here."

Both women looked at her with wide, surprised eyes. "The men are handling everything themselves,"

Sandra said. "There's coffee in the kitchen, if you want a cup."

It was a nice gesture, and Lily flashed Sandra a genuine smile. "Thank you, Sandra. I might just get myself a stout cup of java."

Kevin cleared his throat. Loudly.

"Actually, now that you mention it, Lily, there is something you could help me do."

"Oh?" she asked, genuinely surprised. "What is that?"

Kevin gently detached himself from the women and moved over to Lily, taking her hand and pulling her toward the front door. "I'm so glad you offered."

He didn't say exactly what she had *offered* to do, but her hand was firmly in his so she had to follow.

He didn't slow his pace until they had reached the tree line. Agents were practically swarming the cabin, so Lily felt comfortable stepping into the shadow of the trees a moment, even if she was *un*comfortable being alone once again with Kevin.

Hadn't she promised herself less than an hour ago she wouldn't let such a thing happen? Yet here she was, hand in hand with Kevin, strolling through the woods at an unhurried pace, their silence mutual and surprisingly comfortable.

"What is it you need me for?" she asked when he continued to walk in silence.

He looked down at her and grinned, then turned so he was standing in front of her and took her other hand before she had the slightest notion of his intentions. "Why, to rescue the special agent in distress," he said with a short burst of laughter.

"What agent?" Lily was confused, and a bolt of alarm rang through her. "Is there a problem?"

He reached up and tenderly pushed the hair off her cheek, circling her ear to make sure it stayed. "The only problem is there being too many people in that awfully small cabin."

"They won't be staying," she reminded him. "You're the foreman, after all. You've got it under control," she teased.

"Not the women," he said, shaking his head. "I don't know what to do with them."

She was about to tease him again when she looked into his eyes. He was serious. "You mean you don't *like* all that female attention?"

He shook his head vehemently. "Lily, you know me better than that. There is only *one* woman I want paying attention to me."

Lily swallowed hard, unable to think of anything glib for a reply, and she certainly wasn't going to be honest.

Not even with herself.

She looked away, over Kevin's shoulder, so she wouldn't have to meet his gaze straight on. Still she could feel him watching her, suspecting the heart-flipping half smile lingering on his lips.

After an extended silence, Kevin turned, tucked her hand into the crook of his arm, and began walking slowly down the mountain, picking his steps carefully for both of them. They laughed together at the antics of a couple of chipmunks fighting over a pine nut and stood in awe when they happened upon a herd of elk grazing majestically in a small field.

Finally they stopped by a fallen log in a meadow Lily was sure teemed with wildflowers in the summer and even now, in the dead of winter, had a few colors poking through here and there. Kevin shed his goosedown vest and laid it across the log, urging her to sit on his coat while he took a seat on the bare log next to her.

"I'll bet we've walked a mile already," Lily commented brightly, feeling like she needed to say something but suspecting she was jabbering nonsense. "It's nice out here."

He crossed his arms over the expanse of his chest and nodded. "Very nice."

"Shouldn't we be getting back? I'm sure you're needed to be getting all the equipment organized and the cabin ready for all of Abigail's therapy."

He was silent.

"I'll bet those ladies miss you." She frowned. Now why had she said that?

Kevin tipped his head with a jerk and raised one eyebrow. Not a nod, exactly, but an acknowledgement of her statement nonetheless.

"Where are they staying, by the way? The two women, that is," she clarified. *Not that she cared,* she added silently.

"There's a comfortable two-bedroom cabin at the bottom of the drive."

"I see."

"It's a two-mile driveway," he said dryly, shooting her an amused look.

Lily couldn't help it. Kevin was too charming by half. She chuckled.

Again they sat in silence, each with their own thoughts and relaxed, side by side, not touching but nevertheless aware.

This time, Lily didn't try to fill the silence with unnecessary words. She found they could sit together without speaking and be perfectly comfortable in each other's presence.

"Lily?"

"Hmmm?" she asked, her mind hazy with the surroundings and the moment. His smooth, rich voice didn't quite shatter the stillness she'd been feeling in her heart the last few minutes.

He turned to face her and nudged her chin toward him with his fingertips until their gazes met. His eyes were a bright, sparkling green in the Colorado sunshine, and she couldn't tear her gaze away, found that she didn't really want to. She liked looking into his eyes, liked the warmth she found there.

"Do you believe in love at first sight?" he asked, his voice slipping an octave lower.

"No," Lily replied instantly. "Of course not. There's no such thing. No." She paused, her eyes widening at the meaning of what he *wasn't* saying. "No. I'm not sure I believe in love at all."

He stared at her, mesmerizing her with his gaze. A half smile flickered on his lips and then disappeared, but his eyes continued to glow with emotion.

"I love you, Lily Montague."

"I don't believe you," she said hastily, standing suddenly and taking several steps away from him with her back to him.

He stood and crossed over to her in the swiftness of an instant. She stiffened but did not run, especially when he didn't try to grasp her shoulders and turn her to him. Neither did he try to keep her from moving away from him, though she didn't move a step.

He merely tipped her chin up with his fingertip and turned her head so she could see his face. "I know it's hard to fathom. I can hardly believe it myself."

He reached for her hand and placed a gentle kiss on her fingers.

She made a croaking sound that missed understandable conversation by a mile.

"I'm a man who knows his own mind. And I know I love you, Lily."

She shook her head, trying desperately to deny his

words. Yes, Kevin was as strong and steady a man as she had ever known. She had no doubt at all that he knew what he wanted and would go after his goal until he was successful.

But what he wanted was *her.*

"It can't be."

She turned and began running as fast and as far as she could, her breath coming in short, tight gasps as her feet pounded and slipped across the ground. She could hardly see for the throbbing in her head, and she had no clear idea which way she was going, but she did know it was away from Kevin.

Or at least she thought she was.

He suddenly appeared in front of her when she had been completely certain he was following behind her.

He caught her in his arms, his hands locking around her waist. Then he kissed her.

"Do you realize you're running the wrong way?" he asked, his grin widening. "Another few minutes of jogging and you'll be at Sandra and Marcy's cabin."

She blanched. He always knew what to say to throw her off-kilter.

"What do you want now?" she asked through gritted teeth.

"I want the truth," he said calmly.

"The truth about what?" she snapped, feeling as if she shouldn't have bothered getting up that morning. Everything had gone wrong from the moment she'd set her feet on the rug. From the women in the cabin to Kevin's heart-felt confession, she had been at an extreme disadvantage. Her head was throbbing just thinking about it.

"Look into my eyes and tell me you don't feel the same way I do," he challenged, his grip tightening slightly, as if he was afraid she might run again.

If only he knew. She was in no condition to run. His words had just left her weak in the knees.

She quickly dropped her gaze to the ground, staring at Kevin's sharply polished black boots. She didn't dare look him in the eye at all, for she had no idea of what he might see there.

But she could guess.

"Just look at me and say it, Lily, and then you can walk away. I promise I won't bother you again. I won't say a word about what's happened here."

She remained silent and stiff in his arms. She wished he'd at least let her go so she could breathe, though she knew it was only her own emotional discomfort that was making it feel he was holding her too tight.

"Just say you don't love me, Lily."

She closed her eyes against the nasty pain between her eyebrows. She knew enough about Kevin to know he wasn't going to give up.

So they could just stand there all day, as far as she was concerned, because he wasn't going to get a single word from her on *any* subject.

Lily made it close to another minute before she finally blew out an angry breath and looked up into her tormenter's eyes.

He was still smiling, his eyes gleaming with what she could now brand as love for her, making the moment all the more tenuous. "Well?"

She pinched her lips together, but the words flew from her tongue nonetheless, as if of their own volition. "You know I can't say that."

She felt him visibly relax. "Whew. I'm happy to hear it."

What did he think that meant? It changed nothing between them, not in the terrible version of reality in which they were presently living.

She broke away from him then, turning and walking away at a steady pace without looking back even once to see his reaction.

Suddenly, she stopped. Hands crooked on her hips, she turned around and glared at him.

He was still standing right where she'd left him, his hands tucked in his jeans pockets and a cat-that-ate-the-cream grin on his face.

She made a loud, audible huff which merely made his grin wider. "Which way is the cabin?"

Chapter Nine

Mack knew he'd likely made a tactical error in letting his emotions tumble out of his mouth like a waterfall out of control, and he was sure of it by the time he returned to the cabin.

Lily had now taken over as foreman, and was, in her usual competent way, doing a thorough and meticulous job of it. Physical therapy and exercise machines were being set up in a practical yet eye-pleasing manner, as if they were as much of the interior decoration as the sofa in the middle of the room, and not merely sterile pieces of medical equipment Abby would have to use in order to progress in her health.

Lily even had the two specialists working on the machinery. It gave Kevin pause to admire yet another characteristic in her. He would never have considered on his own asking the degree-possessing ladies to help out with menial tasks.

He had obviously misjudged them. Marcy was wheeling Abby around in the wheelchair, explaining how each piece of equipment worked in great detail. She used a positive and excited voice to tell her how they would help her grow strong and healthy again.

Sandra had a wrench in one hand and a Phillips screwdriver poking out of her back jeans pocket as she helped two agents assemble the parallel bars Abby would use to strengthen her legs. She, too, was smiling, and was chatting happily with the agents. Not only that, she was apparently quite comfortable with hand tools.

Lily was buzzing around like a bee, gently landing here and there, bringing coffee and cookies to the workers and making everyone in the room smile and laugh with her biting wit. Even cantankerous, rusty old agents Mack had known for years were chuckling, men he doubted cracked a smile once in a good month.

She was amazing.

She was also blatantly avoiding him at all costs.

It didn't take a genius to see how she looked everywhere except at him. If he moved one way, she moved the other, though she made her actions appear natural to everyone else in the room. He didn't think a single soul realized how much trouble she was going to in order not to have to speak to him.

Well? What had he honestly expected?

That she'd immediately fall into his arms, all her emotional baggage removed and her sights set on their future together?

He knew better than that. He knew he was going to have to fight her every step of the way.

The truth was he had scared her to death with his mention of love at first sight. It wasn't that she didn't want to believe in it. Didn't every little girl long for a knight to sweep them off their feet someday?

But reality had taken a tough toll on Lily. He was going to have to give her time to get used to the idea of being cherished, safe in a man's arms, and loved as much as life itself.

He knew she felt what was between them—she had admitted as much by being unable to deny it. But she'd been badly hurt by another man and circumstances that never seemed to work in her favor.

Now it was Mack's duty—and his privilege—to coax Lily into the safety of his love. He wouldn't quickly forget the feel of her in his arms, nor the firelight flickering warmly in her eyes as she invited his kiss.

It had taken a great deal of courage on her part to make such a sacrifice. He, better than anyone, knew just how deeply her wounds went, what courage it took simply to respond to his kiss.

She was so tough, so strong and steady on the outside no one would guess how fragile her heart really was. The facade of strength was like a prison wall, if only she knew.

But Mack knew, and he was determined to protect and cherish her—every day for the rest of his life. If only she would let him.

He was a patient man, but he couldn't help but feel frustrated. On the few occasions he'd imagined declaring his love to the woman of his dreams, he'd never pictured that love not being as equally and fiercely requited.

Lily wanted him to back off, and maybe he should, to give her time to recognize her feelings and come to terms with them.

But he'd never been the kind of man to sit on his heels. He was a man of action, and Lily was going to discover just how persistent he could be.

"Looks like you've got things well under control," he complimented as he walked up behind her where she stood sipping a cup of coffee and staring into the fireplace. "I'm impressed."

"Sorry if I took your job away from you," she said stiffly, straightening her posture and grasping the mantle with one hand.

"Oh, no," he assured her, lightly resting his hands on her shoulders. Her muscles were in tight knots as hard as rocks, so he began a gentle massage with his thumbs. "I'm definitely not complaining, especially when you're doing such a great job of it. Better than me, to tell you the truth."

His touch was gentle, more of a caress than a massage, but she jumped away from him as if he'd pinched her. He immediately dropped his hands and frowned, his eyebrows creasing. "What?"

"Excuse me," she mumbled, then strode quickly across the room to her daughter. With a word to Marcy, she took control of the wheelchair and pushed Abby back down the hallway to her bedroom, which was located next to Lily's room and across from Mack's.

Mack watched her until she'd closed the door to Abby's room, scrubbing his head with the fingers of one hand. He did not quite know how to feel.

He did know she was running away from him.

But he was not going to let her.

Nearly two weeks went by without a hitch, Lily thought with satisfaction, watching Marcy manually manipulating Abigail's leg. Progress was much better than expected, really, except for her daughter being unable to provide any useful information on the kidnapped boy.

She felt bad about that. His parents must be out of their minds with worry. At least she had Abigail here with her, even if she was still paralyzed and in a wheelchair. And she was selfishly glad to find no one was pushing Abigail too hard in an attempt to acquire what they needed for poor Jeremy.

Her daughter had quickly slipped into her new routine, and though therapy was often painful, she cheerfully made the best of it. Even school time, with Lily as schoolteacher, was usually a pleasant time for both of them, though she thought perhaps her daughter sometimes got frustrated with her.

It was Lily who was having a tough time making the best of it. She, too, had a routine, but it was not busy enough to suit her.

No matter how hard she worked making lesson plans, teaching Abigail half a day, keeping equipment in order, cooking most of the meals for the agents and medical workers surrounding them, and managing the staff and agents all around the place in her own unique way, it was still not enough.

Not nearly enough to keep her from thinking about Kevin.

No matter what she did, he was in front of her, both literally and figuratively. He didn't attempt to make a lot of personal conversation between them, but kept their encounters straight, to the point, and entirely work-related.

Which, in the most ironic of ways, made her crazy in the head.

That he had stopped asking how she was personally, or cracking the jokes which always made her laugh, didn't seem normal, although she was at a loss as to why she felt that way about it.

This was what she wanted, wasn't it?

For him to leave her to her own life?

She didn't want him pushing her with how he felt

about her. She definitely didn't need him nagging her to know what *her* feelings were about him. She didn't want to go there, and apparently he knew that, and was respecting her wishes by keeping his distance, though not physically, at least emotionally.

Still, she missed the easy camaraderie they'd once shared together. And though Kevin stayed low-key, she knew even Abigail was picking up on the distance which had suddenly grown between them. Her little girl hadn't said anything, but Lily saw the strange looks she gave when Kevin suddenly and abruptly turned in another direction upon spying Lily, and how he never made time for the three of them together anymore.

She hated to hurt Abigail with her own personal problems. Maybe she would talk to Kevin about that, at least.

Right now it was too late to talk to anyone about anything. She was just turning in for another long, sleepless night. She'd never tossed around at night so much in her life, not even in the midst of a fever. And when she dreamed, it was even worse.

Daydreams became nightmares. She couldn't hold her feelings at bay when she was asleep.

But it was waking up that hurt the worst. To discover in the cold, hard light of morning that she wasn't in Kevin's strong arms with a ring on her finger to proclaim her his wife. That her dreams of the night past were just that—dreams.

She pulled on a sweatsuit and a heavy pair of socks, then slipped under the covers. The cabin was heated only by the fire and the nights were cold.

She pulled the covers up to her chin and turned on her side, reaching to turn off the light on the nightstand. When she spied a well-worn Bible lying on the stand she changed her mind and left the light on, reaching for the worn book instead.

How had it gotten here?

She scooted herself up to a sitting position, bunching two pillows behind her for support, then began flipping slowly through the Bible. The pages were bent and bruised from heavy reading, and she noticed some verses carefully underlined, obviously with the use of a straight-edged instrument.

It had been a long, long time since she'd picked up a Bible.

Suddenly she wanted to read something, but wasn't sure where to start. She didn't think just opening the Good Book to a random page was such a good idea, and neither was starting at the beginning of Genesis.

Somewhere in God's Word, she knew, was a measure of comfort. Not the answer to all her problems, maybe, but she could use some divine reassurance right now, as much as she ever had.

She closed the Bible and tapped her index finger against the worn brown leather cover, thinking back to her childhood, when the Bible was a near and dear friend to her.

Of course! The Psalms. The poetry would be enjoyable to read, even if she didn't find any personal comfort.

She recalled how her second-grade Sunday-school teacher Mrs. Brighton explained to her small charges, including Lily, how to find the Psalms.

"Put your finger right there in the middle of the Bible," Mrs. Brighton said in her crackly, ancient-sounding voice. *"Then open your Bible wide. Surprise. You've found the Psalms."*

Lily chuckled to herself as she poked her finger into the middle section of the Bible and opened it up.

The Psalms. Imagine that.

With a contented sigh, she pulled the covers back up around her chin again and began reading, starting at Psalms One. Intrigued, she continued.

Two hours had passed before she realized she'd read through the entire book of Psalms, when she had originally just planned to browse over them.

And there were tears in her eyes.

God had, indeed, provided a sense of peace to her aching heart. She had shunned Him when her husband died, but reading through the Psalms, she realized God had never left her—not throughout all her agonizing adult life nor all the tragedies she and her family had been through. And not now, not even with this kidnapping and Abigail being hurt so terribly.

For the first time, she sensed a higher purpose to

what was going on around her, and the thought made her heart beat faster with excitement.

God had a plan. And oh—*how* she needed someone wiser to have a good plan.

She was no longer tired, but she slid deeper into bed and cradled the soft leather Bible to her heart, crossing her arms over her chest and hugging the beloved book to herself.

Maybe somehow, with God's help, she could work her mess of a life out. With God's help, Abigail could be healed and whole again—physically and emotionally.

And Kevin...

She closed her eyes and, for the first time in years, began to tentatively pray about all the worries in her heart. And to thank God for all the joy she had experienced through the pain.

Suddenly she heard the oddest sound, so strange, that it made her pop out of bed, frowning and cocking her ear.

What *was* that?

It sounded like *music*.

Guitar music, to be exact. And it was coming from the vicinity of her window.

She glanced at her clock. She knew she hadn't gone to bed early, and she had to have spent hours reading the Psalms. She couldn't imagine anyone was still up at this hour.

Why, it was past eleven o'clock. Who would be blasting music at this time of night?

After pacing around her room a couple of times, she cautiously made her way to the window. When she pulled back the curtains covering the sliding glass door leading out onto a covered porch, it occurred to her she'd not spent time out there during her stay. There was a chair out there, though that wasn't what had caught Lily's interest.

Past the porch, in the shadow of a pine tree, a lone guitarist strummed boldly and loudly. Whoever it was, he was good, even if it was the wrong time of day—night—to be showing his skills off. Every note was carefully plucked or strummed, and it sounded as if he had quite the repertoire as one song changed rapidly to another without missing a beat, classical to jazz with a stroke of his pick.

She could not make out his face, but his shape was familiar, and she felt her throat tighten in response to the unexpected serenade.

With a burst of song coming from his lips, Kevin stepped out into the full moonlight. Lily's mouth gaped open at the audacity of the man.

He was singing a love song, some Broadway melody she halfway recognized but couldn't quite place. His voice was rich and deep, and so full of emotion he brought a tear to the corner of her eye.

It wasn't so much the words, though the sweet, slow ballad was beautiful. It wasn't the guitar, either, though Kevin played with such ease and precision she knew it had to be a natural talent he hadn't mentioned possessing.

But it was the mysterious, disturbing emotional bass of his voice that wrapped around her heart and pulled at everything inside her. It was like a smoky haze that crept up and surrounded her, slowly spinning round and round about her until her skin prickled with the sensation of music itself.

When the song was over, Kevin stopped playing and hung the guitar over his shoulder at his right side. His eyes gleamed in the moonlight.

Lily couldn't move. She couldn't breathe. She could only stare at him in awe.

He chuckled and shook his head at her. "Haven't you ever been serenaded before, sweetheart?"

She broke free of the enchantment and folded her arms across her chest. "As a matter of fact, no, I have not," she said, surprised at how keen and precise her voice sounded, when inside she was shaking. "Most particularly not at eleven o'clock at night. Kevin, you've probably awakened everyone in a four-mile radius."

He walked up to the rail and leaned on it, closing his gaze in on hers and freezing her to the spot. "I don't care."

She raised her eyebrows over her ever-widening eyes. She honestly didn't know what to say, and that was a first for her.

Kevin leaned forward on his arms. "I don't care if everyone in the world hears how I feel about you, Lily. I'll yell it from the highest mountain if I have to, in order to get your attention."

"Please don't," she said crisply, brushing a nervous hand through her long black hair.

"Why not?"

He jumped over the railing with both feet together, like something out of a movie, managing not to smash his guitar, which still hung untarnished at his side. His movements were as smooth as an animal's—a predator, she suspected.

Leaning against the rail, he mimicked Lily, crossing his arms and tipping his chin in the air.

His grin was the real killer, though.

Lily thought she'd never seen such an attractive man in her life. His black jeans and tight black T-shirt were now familiar to her, but at the moment they were ach-ingly alluring.

She closed her eyes, trying to regain her equilibrium, but she still felt dizzy and her emotions quite out of control.

After a moment, she opened her eyes and met his green-eyed gaze. "Kevin, what are you trying to do?" she asked, her voice tight.

"I'm serenading your great beauty," he teased, placing a hand over his heart. "A tribute to the love I feel for you."

"Don't be silly," she snapped, affected far more by his words than she wanted to admit. "No one serenades anyone anymore."

The smile left his face and his eyes blazed. "I just did."

"Yes, you did," she admitted with a curt nod. "And I

have to admit it was very romantic. But you have to stop this nonsense."

He shook his head. "Not until you tell me you feel the same way I do." He stroked his jaw as he slowly looked her over, head to foot. "I'm quite serious, Lily. I love you, and I'm going to show you how I feel every time I have the opportunity."

Terrific. That was exactly what she *didn't* want to hear. If she hadn't gotten through to him by now, how on earth was she going to get out of this predicament without hurting him?

She did care about Kevin, enough to want to spare his hurt feelings.

"Kevin," she said, moving to lean on the rail beside him. "The truth is, it doesn't matter how I feel. It doesn't matter how you feel. Nothing can happen between us. There are too many circumstances against us. Surely you see that."

"I see the barriers you're putting up," he acknowledged. "But haven't you every heard the phrase *love conquers all?*"

"Love *doesn't* conquer all, Kevin," she said sharply. "I'm bruised but living proof of that."

"But you can try again."

"I have a daughter to think about, and I'm thinking about her right now."

"Lily," he said, his voice gruff with emotion. "I love Abby, too. You know that."

"Yes," she said softly. "But that's not the issue. I need to concentrate my full energy on getting her well and, God willing, walking again."

"And I need the information she has on the kidnapper, when she's strong enough to talk about it."

Lily nodded fiercely. "Exactly. We both have jobs to do. Important jobs that have to come first, before our feelings. We have to keep our focus completely on our true goals."

"So you do have feelings for me," he said, reaching his hand out to push the hair away from her cheek.

Lily just looked at him, aghast.

"I can't ignore what I'm feeling. I'm in love with you. I think about you all the time. I can't live without you."

Lily felt her throat close until she felt like choking. "You won't be. I'm no further than the next room, for pity's sake."

"That's not what I mean and you know it." It was the first time his voice had sounded strained since the beginning of their conversation.

They were quiet for a moment, each, Lily thought, firming up their own arguments.

"What difference does it make, anyway?" she continued, hoping her rational arguments would win over his powerful emotional appeals. "When you have the information you want, you're going to leave. You have no choice in the matter."

He stared at her, his face grim and his lips a solemn line. He gave a quick, curt nod that Lily almost missed, then gravely said, "You're right."

Chapter Ten

Mack was stymied. He'd given it his best shot, and Lily had not been impressed. If anything, she'd been put out by his antics.

He flipped through the paperwork scattered across his bed and chuckled out loud. Perhaps serenading Lily hadn't been the brightest idea of his life, but it had seemed like the right thing to do at the time.

And she *had* called it romantic—just before she'd begged him to stop.

He'd been speaking with Marcy and Sandra, and both had informed him Abby was close to a breakthrough. He thought so, too, but he was waiting for some sign from her that she was truly strong enough before he pushed her, before he asked her make the horrifying and painful journey back to the terrifying day she'd been paralyzed.

In the meantime, he'd thought of a new way to approach Lily, something she'd said some time ago back at the Montague mansion on the day of the picnic. He hoped this time it would work.

He pulled a flannel shirt on over his T-shirt, buttoned it quickly and tucked it into his jeans. Hastily, he threw a black down vest around his shoulders and grunted in satisfaction. Today, he wore scuffed black snakeskin cowboy boots instead of his usual spit-polished military boots.

After a quick look in the mirror where he brushed an unruly lock of hair out of his face with his fingers, he took a deep breath and went to find Lily.

She was with Abby, crouched beside the wheelchair and explaining how the leg braces Marcy held in her hands would help her walk in a shorter amount of time. How they were necessary for her healing.

"But they're so *ugly,* Mom," Abby protested, crossing her arms with a huff.

The child's eyes lit up when Mack walked into the room, and he grinned and moved to her side, kneeling on the other side of her chair. "What's up, kiddo?" he asked with a laugh.

"Tell her," Abby demanded. "Tell my mom these things are horrible. Everyone will be staring at me if I put them on."

Mack restrained the chuckle on his lips and met Lily's gaze. She rolled her eyes in exasperation. "Can *you* talk some sense into her?" she begged.

"See how stubborn she is?" Abby said, waving an

arm toward her mother. "I told you. She's being completely unreasonable."

"Well now, Abby," Mack said, stroking his chin with his thumb and forefinger. "We already knew your mother was stubborn."

"Kevin," Lily protested. "You are not helping out here."

Mack disagreed. He had Abby laughing, and that was a good start. He stood and gave Abby a hug. "Seriously, sweetie, your mother is right. At least this one time, she is." He winked at Lily.

She frowned, but he had Abby's rapt attention, so he continued. "They don't look as bad on, I promise. And there isn't a man or woman here who would consider you ugly."

He took the girl's face in both hands and met her gaze squarely. He wanted to be sure she could see the truth of his words deep in his eyes. "You are the most beautiful little girl I know. If I had a little girl of my own, I would want her to be just like you."

"You would?" Abby still didn't sound convinced, but she was breaking.

"Cross my heart," he said, using his forefinger to line a big X on his chest.

"Even in this wheelchair?"

"Even so."

"Even with these ugly braces on my legs?"

"Even more, then, Abby, because those braces show how strong and brave you are."

He wasn't prepared for the girl to throw her arms around his neck and plant a big, smacking kiss on his unshaven cheek. He nearly somersaulted over her wheelchair, but even worse, his heart took a whopping tumble around in his chest.

Even when he'd righted himself, he still felt dizzy, and he knew his face was flame-red.

"I love you, Abby," he said, his voice gruff with emotion.

"I love you, too, Kevin," the girl replied with a bright smile. Then she turned to her mother. "Okay," she said with a loud sigh, "Let's get these ugly things on my legs and get on with it."

Lily turned the wheelchair and wheeled it to where Marcy sat on the couch. "Can you help Abigail with these braces, Marcy?" she asked crisply. "I'll be back in a moment."

She patted Abby on the arm and then turned toward Mack. It was only then that he saw her face was as red as his had been moments earlier.

She walked straight to him and grabbed his sleeve, gripping it in a fist as she whirled him toward the door and whisked him out into the morning sunshine.

She did not stop until they were well past the tree line, where she abruptly stopped and turned on him. He could practically see smoke furling from her ears.

He braced himself for who knew what.

"You're *leaving,*" she accused, harshly and rather loudly.

"What?" He had no idea what she was talking about, but whatever it was, it was serious to her.

She stepped forward, poking him in the chest with her index finger. "Don't you know what you've just done?"

He shook his head, speechless.

"You told Abigail you love her."

Lily made it sound as though he'd just threatened her daughter with some awful crime. He shrugged. "I do love Abby."

"Oh," she growled, her fists in a ball. "Are you really that heartless? You told her you love her, and then you're going to leave."

Finally, Mack was beginning to see where she was going with this. She still didn't believe that he could leave to perform his FBI duties and then return again to love and take care of them.

And she had good reason to doubt. But he didn't know how to convince her he would be back.

"I'm not going anywhere," he said firmly.

"No, maybe not now. Maybe not today, or even this week. But when you have the information you need, you'll leave, all right."

He gave a curt nod to acknowledge the truth. "But I will be back."

"Sure you will." Bitterness lined her voice as she looked away from him.

"I *will*," he assured her, but he knew she didn't believe him. He could see it in her eyes, in the tenseness of her shoulders.

"I *will*," he said again, lacing his words with every bit of honesty he possessed, and feeling ridiculously as if he was reciting wedding vows.

He took her hand, the one she was poking into his chest, and held it tenderly before him, quickly covering it with his other hand and stroking back and forth with his thumb.

"I will come back. And if you move or run away, I'll just follow you and find you. Don't you see?"

She looked away, unable to keep his gaze. "I know you feel like that now, Kevin," she said softly. She sounded as if she might be in tears, but he doubted it.

Not Lily.

"But once you're gone…" The words drifted off into nothingness.

"Let's talk about something else," he suggested, knowing there were no words to convince her.

She would simply have to see for herself when the time came.

"Yes," she agreed. "We really ought to get back to Abigail. She'll be wondering where we are."

"She knows where we are," he said.

"What?"

"I have to admit I enlisted her as a co-conspirator in my plan."

She narrowed her eyes, but the tenseness was gone from her face. "What does that mean? Why do I think I should be running away?"

He chuckled. "No need to take flight. This is a good kind of surprise."

"Surprise?" Her eyes lit up, and he laughed again.

"So you like surprises, do you?" he asked.

"What woman doesn't?"

"Yes, but you're not just any woman."

"What's my surprise?" Eagerness had returned to her voice, and her cheeks were now rosy with anticipation instead of anger.

He took the hand he still held in his and turned, lacing his fingers with hers as he began walking down the mountain. "Come with me, and you'll see," he promised.

Lily was still struggling with her emotions, but she allowed Kevin to pull her down the hillside. She didn't believe for one moment that there was any kind of future for the two of them. And she wouldn't even allow herself to put a name on her own feelings.

She knew Kevin believed what he said. But she knew better. She hoped now he at least knew not to push Abigail into this. Her daughter didn't need someone to love her and leave her at her tender age, especially considering the circumstances.

Abigail knew Kevin wouldn't be there forever. She was a smart little girl, and Lily prayed she would not be unintentionally hurt by all this.

Somehow, she doubted it. She, herself, would be hurt, and she knew exactly what was going on. She had been here before.

How could her young daughter possibly weather it?

She was still considering this when Kevin stopped suddenly, still within the tree line. He turned to face her eagerly.

"Close your eyes," he said, stepping behind her and placing his palms over her eyes.

"What? Come on, Kevin."

"Just humor me."

She sighed loudly. "Okay, my eyes are closed. Now what?"

"Start walking. Straight forward."

Lily put her hands in front of her, feeling young and vulnerable. Excitement welled in her chest despite her best efforts to keep it at bay.

"Can I look yet?" she asked when she felt she'd been walking forever.

"Not yet. Keep walking."

"Now?" she asked impatiently after a few more steps.

"No. Keep walking."

"Now?"

"No…no…okay, now *look*."

She'd never heard him so excited, and she quickly opened her eyes.

At the bottom of the hill they stood on was a small stable. They were still far enough off and the wind blowing the right way that Lily hadn't detected the scent of hay and horses, which was one of her favorite smells in the whole world.

In the corral, two horses were saddled and tied to the fence by their halters.

Kevin laughed. "Do you like it?"

She looked up at him, feeling suddenly shy. "Are we going to go riding?" she asked, holding her breath for the answer.

"If I'm not mistaken, those two horses in the corral have our names on them."

She couldn't help it. She squealed and threw her arms around his neck. "This is a dream come true. I've always wanted to go riding, but Mama never let me."

He chuckled as he whirled her around and set her down again. "I remember."

"What?"

"At our little indoor picnic. You told me the story of how your mother didn't trust horses and never let you take lessons."

"I had to take ballet lessons," she said, making a face. "I even had to do this dance with my teddy bear. Oh, it was awful. *I* was awful."

"Hmm, yes," he said thoughtfully. "I think you said that, too. Well, you can't be good at everything, sweetheart. I'll bet you'll look great on the back of a horse, though."

She smiled. "Oh, I hope so."

Kevin gestured to the stable. "There's one way to find out."

He held his hand out to her and she didn't hesitate before taking it. Moments later they were in the corral with the horses.

"Put your foot in the stirrup and I'll lift you up," he commanded.

A moment later, she was sitting high in the saddle. It felt as if she'd been there all her life. She wasn't the least bit frightened, only excited. She tried to calm herself, knowing the horse could pick up on her feelings.

"I hope you like buckskins," Kevin said, mounting his own horse, a beautiful black Percheron with lovely feathering at her feet.

Lily's buckskin was a fine dark-golden color with a black mane and tail. She couldn't have picked a better horse in her dreams.

"What's her name?" she asked as a stablehand bridled the horse. The horse sidestepped and snorted.

Kevin laughed. "I think you've offended him. He's a boy, and his name is Gaylan."

"And yours?"

He shook his head and sighed. "Her name is Angel. Let's hope she lives up to that reputation."

The stablehand handed Lily the reins. "Left for left, right for right, back for whoa and keep the reins loose otherwise," he instructed sounding as if he were reciting a familiar litany.

"That sounds easy enough," she said, eager to get onto a mountain trail. "Kevin, lead the way."

Lily found her horse followed Kevin's mount without much effort on her part, so she could enjoy the scenery as they followed the trail up into national park grounds. She was enthralled by the trees and the small animals foraging for food, but most of all, the snow.

The snow made everything around them beautiful. It glistened in the sunlight and made even ugly vales and dead trees look lovely.

They rode in silence for a long time, then Kevin turned his horse sideways across the trail. Lily pulled back on the reins, and Gaylan raised his front legs a little and snorted in indignation.

"Not so hard," Kevin coached. "Give him a light hand on the reins.

Coloring, Lily loosened her grip. At least she hadn't lost her seat when her horse reared up. That counted for something, didn't it?

"What do you think of your first ride?" he asked, grinning.

"This is perfect. Do you think we could run with the horses a little bit?"

He chuckled. "You've got a great seat, but I'm not sure about *running,* as you put it. How about a nice, easy trot for starters?"

He turned his horse and nudged her with his heels. "C'mon, Angel, let's see what you can do." As Angel moved into a trot, he turned in the saddle and called back, "Ride with your knees and thighs. Don't clutch the saddle horn if you can avoid it."

Gaylan followed Angel into a trot without any urging. The trot was a lot different than she imagined. Her horse's smooth walk turned into a four-point bounce with her on every corner.

Lily grabbed desperately for the saddle horn. She was bouncing all over the saddle and had lost her footing in the left stirrup.

"Kevin!" she called frantically. He had pulled far ahead of her and was trotting off into an open meadow.

He reined in immediately and turned his horse in her direction. He was laughing as he approached.

"Knees and thighs, remember?" he called.

She reined in clumsily. "What, exactly does that mean?"

"Don't ride the horse. Feel the horse. You should feel as if you are an extension of Gaylan, not an appendage sitting on his back."

"Okay," she said hesitantly. She had no idea what Kevin was talking about, but she was, quite literally, along for the ride.

"Let me show you," he offered, patting Angel on the neck. "Keep a good rein on Gaylan so he doesn't follow me."

Lily took a good grip on the reins and prayed her horse wouldn't move.

"Get up, Angel," Kevin called, then nudged his horse into a smooth canter.

She could see what he meant about being one with the horse. He and Angel flowed seamlessly together. There was no doubt he was holding his seat, and even the horse appeared to be enjoying herself.

He rode past her and yelled, "Watch this."

Angel took off like a bullet and flew across the meadow at full gallop. Kevin's thick dark-brown hair was whipping back as he leaned forward in the saddle, one hand waving in the air and looking every bit the old Western cowboy.

Lily couldn't breathe. She forgot all about being on a horse as she watched him manipulate faulty ground and leap over fallen logs. Man and animal were magnificent to behold.

She had trouble speaking when he finally reined to a halt before her. "I never knew…"

"I'll buy you a horse," he said with a smile. "A buckskin, if you like."

"Don't be ridiculous," she said, turning her gaze away from his.

"You'll see," he promised. "You'll *see* about a lot of things."

She didn't know what he meant, so she didn't comment. She merely nudged her horse around heading back the way they came. "We ought to be getting back to the stable, don't you think?"

"Can we do one thing first?" he asked, his voice low and velvet-soft.

"Sure."

"It's corny, but I've seen it in the movies dozens of times and I've always wondered if it could be done in real life."

Now she was worried. "What is that?"

He nudged his horse up next to hers, so they were riding side by side. "Hold hands with me."

"On a horse?" she exclaimed.

"It will fulfill a dream of mine," he coaxed in a voice she couldn't refuse.

"What? To see me fall off this horse flat on my backside?"

He chuckled. "You won't fall. I promise."

For some unknown reason, she believed him and reached for his open hand.

"Okay, now," she said, concentrating on *knees and thighs.* "This seems to be okay."

"Good," Kevin said, nudging his mare into a quick trot.

"Kevin!" Lily shrieked as Gaylan followed suit, rapidly trotting to catch up with Angel. Amazingly, her hand was still in his.

And she had *not* fallen off the horse.

As they trotted along, side by side, holding hands, she suddenly realized she wasn't thinking about riding anymore. She *was* riding.

"Woo-hoo!" she shouted, squeezing Kevin's hand in

elation. This was what she'd always thought horseback riding would be like. She couldn't remember laughing so much as she did on that trail.

Suddenly, Kevin reigned in, pulling his horse close beside hers and blocking Gaylan from movement.

"There's one more thing," he said, grinning mysteriously.

"Another dream of yours?" she asked, rolling her eyes and laughing. "Something you've seen dozens of times in the movies?"

"You could say that." He reached a hand out and slipped his fingers behind her jaw, gently drawing her toward him. By the time she realized what he wanted, it was too late to do anything about it.

He swept a soft, gentle kiss across her lips, and then followed that motion with the pad of his thumb.

"There," he said, his voice husky. "Now this day really is perfect."

Chapter Eleven

Mack was in for a surprise of his own when he returned to the cabin, but not nearly the shock he knew Lily experienced.

They walked in the front door together, laughing and clowning around, when Adora Montague stepped from the hallway and loomed over them, giving each of them a severe look Mack humorously imagined was her closest attempt at a welcome.

"Mother," Lily squeaked, immediately stiffening. All the work Mack had done that afternoon to loosen her up was gone in an instant. "What are you doing here?"

"Visiting my daughter and granddaughter," she said crisply. "What did you think I was doing?"

"Well, we're very glad to see you," Mack said, extending his hand to her. "Aren't we, Lily?"

He playfully nudged Lily with his shoulder when

she remained silent. "Of course," she replied belatedly, stumbling over her words.

"I didn't bring a housemaid and I haven't finished unpacking," Adora said, waving her arm vaguely toward the hallway. "Can I steal Lily away for a few minutes in order to help me, Kevin?"

He noticed she used his cover name. Adora had been calling him Mack since Day One, but now it was *Kevin*. He suspected she was trying to make things easier for Lily.

The old woman had a gruff exterior, but he was beginning to think there was a heart in there somewhere. Adora's kindness was more subtle, rather than the blatant type he himself preferred.

He looked down at Lily and winked. "Oh, I'm sure she'd love to help out."

Lily met his gaze and rolled her eyes. "Oh, thank you," she said for his ears only.

Mack chuckled.

Marcy and Sandra were nowhere to be seen, but Abby had wheeled her chair to the far window and was staring out with a distant look on her face.

"Hey, love, what are you doing?" he asked, crouching beside her chair to put an arm around her tiny shoulders. She still seemed so small, so weak and vulnerable, and Mack experienced a protective tug in his chest. He'd never imagined a child could do so much to a man, particularly one as gruff and unfeeling as he was.

"Looking for animals," she informed him.

"See any?"

"No. Not one. Why aren't there any televisions up here?"

He wasn't about to tell the little girl the truth, that they didn't want her accidentally to pick up a news program on the kidnapping which might frighten her and set her back.

"That's just the way it has to be for a little while, kiddo. Think you can handle it?"

She shrugged. "I guess. I'm bored, though."

"Well, that," he said with a smile as he ruffled her hair with his palm, "I can do something about. Do you play checkers?"

He walked to the hall closet and pulled out a board. "I'm warning you, I'm a mean checkers player."

"You're not mean, Kevin."

He chuckled at her misinterpretation. And it turned out to be true, even if it wasn't in the way Abby meant when she said it.

She beat him three out of four games.

Fair and square.

He was actually relieved when Adora came down the hallway. He wasn't sure his ego could stand another brutal loss.

"May I interrupt you?" Adora asked as if it was already done. "I need to speak to my granddaughter for a moment."

Mack stood and pulled out the chair he'd been sitting on while playing checkers with Abby. With a grand sweep of his hand, he gestured for Adora to have a seat and made sure she was comfortable before speaking.

"I have some paperwork to catch up on in my bedroom," he said, gathering up the checkers and the board. "Can I get you anything before I leave?"

"No, but thank you," Adora said primly. "I believe my granddaughter and I will be just fine on our own for a few minutes."

"Okay, then," he said, winking at Abby. "I'll leave you to it."

He moved toward the hallway, stopping to put the checkerboard away. He didn't mean to listen in on their conversation, but Adora's voice, even when she was speaking in a whisper, carried easily across the room to where he was standing.

"You and I, Abigail, must become co-conspirators," she said, laying a tender hand on Abby's hair and stroking it softly.

Mack couldn't help it. His inherent training took over. His ears pricked up and adrenaline rushed through his veins.

Co-conspirators?

She had his attention.

He quietly closed the closet door and walked casually down the hallway, then crouched and closed back in so he could continue to overhear the conversation in the great room.

It occurred to him that what he was doing was wrong,

but though he knew curiosity killed the cat, he couldn't help himself. Stuffy old Adora getting into mischief was just a bit more than he could handle on any occasion, especially this one.

"What do you mean, *Grand-mère?*" Abby said excitedly, her hands waving.

Mack crouched down more and leaned farther in to hear her answer.

"It's Kevin and your mother I'm talking about," Adora said shortly. "We have to do something about the two of them."

Mack smothered a chuckle. What had he done now, that deserved Adora's attention?

Abby knew. "They love each other," she squealed, sounding very happy about it.

Mack was glad for that.

"Correct, child," Adora agreed mildly. "You are very perceptive."

Abby grinned at *Grand-mère*'s subtle praise. Mack suspected she didn't hear it very often.

"Dear heart," Adora said, suddenly quiet and very serious. "I need to know how you feel."

"'Bout what?" Abby queried. "I feel good. Kevin and Mom take care of me."

"No, no," said Adora with what Mack thought might be a light chuckle. "I mean about your mother. About Kevin being a permanent part of your life."

Heat rushed to Mack's face.

"I love Kevin."

The statement was so honest and sincere, in the way only a child could make it, that tears sprung to Mack's eyes. He was not a man to cry. Not at funerals, and not at the horrors he'd seen on the job.

Over the years, he'd purposefully toughened his heart not to feel too deeply about anything. How could he not, with the job he had?

But now, his heart was touched in a way he'd never known before. He wanted to call out that he loved Abby, too, but that would give him away, so he remained silent, crouched in the hallway with his chest tight and his tear ducts stinging.

That blessed little girl. He would have to give her an extra hug or two later, just so she knew how he felt about her, even if he couldn't tell her.

He remembered Lily's warning about what he said and did with Abby, but Lily didn't understand. He wouldn't hurt the little girl.

Lily didn't know he meant what he said. He *would* return. He *would* make them a family.

Because he knew he couldn't live without that stubborn woman and her adorable little girl.

Despite the emotion weighing down his chest, he nearly snickered at Adora's next words.

"Abigail, you know your mother can be mulish, not to mention her tendency to overlook the obvious. Isn't that right, dear?"

Abby laughed. "Oh, *Grand-mère*. You're so funny when you talk about Mom."

"She *is* a trial," Adora defended with a haughty sniff. "If only you knew."

"Why do we have to be co-consir...conspira...conspirata-tationers?"

"Conspirators," the old woman corrected crisply. "That means we need to work together toward a common cause."

"Why?"

"Because, dear heart," the old woman said smoothly, "I don't believe Kevin and your mother have the slightest chance at happiness unless the two of us interfere and help them."

She paused and leaned in farther. "We have to play Cupid, Abigail," she said in what was almost a stage whisper. "Do you know what that means?"

"That means my mom isn't going to go out with Kevin, even if she loves him in her heart."

Mack pinched his lips together. Hard. The kid was really with it, that one.

"Precisely," Adora agreed. "Though I do think, to give him credit, we have Kevin on our side. He really seems to be working on their relationship. I feel sorry for the poor man."

This time Mack had to slap his hand over his mouth to keep from making a sound. Not good for a special agent with Army Ranger training.

"What are we going to do, *Grand-mère?*" Abby asked, her voice raising in excitement.

Mack dropped down to his knees and crawled silently down the hallway toward his bedroom.

The spying ended here. He couldn't imagine what the two wily females would concoct, and he wasn't sure he wanted to find out.

The following afternoon, Lily was looking for Abigail and was alarmed when she couldn't find her anywhere in the cabin. She searched the child's bedroom, the great room, and even, after knocking, took a quick peek into Kevin's bedroom, all to no avail.

Now, alarm was changing to panic. Marcy and Sandra had said nothing of an excursion, and her mother was napping in her bedroom.

The only ones missing from the cabin were Abigail and...*Kevin.*

Suddenly she knew with a blessed assuredness that Abigail was safe with Kevin. Where they were she had no guess, and she definitely planned to chew him out for not telling her where he was taking the small girl, but she completely trusted him to take care of her daughter.

Deciding to wait on the porch, she grabbed the mystery novel she was in the midst of reading and nodded to the two special agents stationed at the front door. There was an old wooden swing to the left side of the door, and after testing the chains to make certain they would hold, she sat down and curled her feet under her, quickly losing herself in the plot of the book, the occasional cool breeze touching the back of her neck a welcome change of pace from the fire that always roared within the fireplace in the cabin.

"Mom!"

Lily raised her head to see Kevin trudging up the road, Abigail tucked safely in his arms. He didn't look as if he was straining a bit having to carry the girl, though Lily imagined he'd been walking for some time.

When they reached the porch, Kevin tucked Abigail on the swing next to Lily and stood, leaning his shoulder against a convenient post. His breath was coming fast, and he wiped the edge of his black denim sleeve across his forehead. The other hand he kept hidden behind his back, a stance Lily assumed had something to do with his military training.

"Whew," he said with a huff of breath. "That's quite a walk."

"Where did you go?" she asked curiously, raising her eyebrows at Kevin and letting him know by the strength of her gaze this question was far from her last word on the subject.

He made the slightest of nods to acknowledge the unspoken message and said, "Abby, why don't you tell your mom what we did?"

"Oh, Mom, it was wonderful," Abigail gushed.

"Kevin said I could use some fresh air, and he took me down the road to a pretty meadow."

"Carried you all that way, did he?" she said, a subtle jab at Kevin.

"Kevin has huge muscles in his arms," Abigail said. "You should feel them."

Kevin chuckled loudly and flexed his biceps on one arm with a big wink at Lily.

"Thank you, no," she responded, feeling as though she'd eaten a big spoonful of peanut butter, the way her tongue was sticking to the roof of her mouth.

Kevin made another pose with his arm, this time downward. "You're sure?"

It was too ridiculous not to laugh, and her chuckle made Kevin's smile even larger.

"Ke-vin," Abigail said, widening her eyes at the man and gesturing secretively.

Lily's gaze bore down on her daughter, but Abigail only batted her eyelashes innocently and flashed her a guilty smile.

Hmm. Yes. Some innocent.

Those two were up to something, and Lily was going to find out what it was, by whatever means necessary, the first being the direct approach.

"What are you two up to?" she asked, leveling each of them with her gaze.

Both were silent, eyeing each other as if trying to communicate that way.

"Spit it out," she demanded. "You know I'm going to find out anyway, so you might as well just save yourself the trouble and tell me now."

"Kevin forgot something," Abigail said meaningfully, trying to wink at the man but actually blinking.

"That I did," he agreed, giving Abigail a fond grin that then widened to include Lily.

"What? In the field?" she asked.

"It was a meadow, mom," Abigail corrected.

"Meadow, field, whatever. What did you forget?" She turned her gaze toward Kevin.

"Well, it's not like that, exactly," he said, hedging and clearing his throat.

"Oh, I see," she said, though she did not. "What, exactly, is it like, then, if you don't mind telling me that?"

"Ke-e-vin!" Abigail sounded thoroughly exasperated with her burly companion.

"Oh, all right then." His face flushed red as he pulled his arm from behind his back.

He was holding a bouquet of fresh-picked wildflowers. Kneeling before her to be eye-and-eye, he offered her the colorful collection.

"You picked these for me?" She found herself oddly flattered. She'd often been the recipient of expensive bouquets of roses, but never had anyone taken the time to pick her flowers before.

Especially in the snow.

"And it took him a long time, too," Abigail said, confirming her thoughts. "There aren't very many flowers in the winter. But Kevin worked real hard and got some for you."

Lily looked at him. For once in her life, she wasn't sure what to do or say. "Um, thank you, Kevin. The flowers are lovely. Maybe I should go put them in water before they wilt."

Kevin raised his hands. "Oh, no. Not yet, you're not."

"Why not?"

Kevin leaned forward and tilted his head to one side, tapping on his freshly shaven cheek. "Plant me a little one right here, and then I'll let you go fix your flowers however you want."

Abigail laughed and clapped, earning her a stern look from Lily, which the girl ignored.

This was not funny. Lily hated it when Kevin forced her hand. What's more, it was undignified. There was no way to leave this situation with grace.

With a loud sigh which she hoped told Kevin exactly what she thought about this little shenanigan, she leaned forward and puckered her lips, smacking a loud but brief kiss on his cheek.

His musky aftershave followed her back to her sitting position, and she had made the mistake of placing her hand on his "big muscles," as Abby called them, to balance herself when she leaned forward.

She had to admit, Kevin was attractive. Attractive in

more ways than Lily could count, the best of which was his giving heart.

But she thought he probably knew it.

And if he did, he was using it against her.

"Mom! Kevin!" Abigail sounded anxious, and they both turned.

"What's wrong, love?" Kevin asked softly, reaching for her hand.

Lily gave him a stern warning look for his careless words. "Are you uncomfortable?" she asked her daughter. "Should we bring you inside?"

Abigail nodded. "Actually, I would like to go inside. But I'm not tired."

Kevin obliged, standing to his feet and scooping Abigail into his arms. "Where do you want to go, lo—er—Abby?"

Abigail looked at Lily and smiled. The little girl had the oddest light in her eyes, as if she was planning something. Lily hoped not, for her own sake.

"I would like to work on the parallel bars. I'm feeling strong today."

"That's great, hon," Lily exclaimed.

"But I need both of you to help me. I can't do it by myself."

Lily thought one or the other of them would be plenty, but she went along with her daughter's request. And Kevin readily agreed, whirling the child around and seeming nearly as excited as Abigail.

"Let's go, Mom," Kevin said with a wink. "We don't want her to change her mind when she's in such a good mood, do we?"

"Yes, but what's putting that sneaky daughter of mine in such a good mood, I'm wondering," she said, tickling Abigail in the ribs. "Why do I get the distinct impression I'm being set up?"

She leveled her gaze on Kevin. If there was a plot, he would definitely be a part of it. He and Abigail had probably spent the morning figuring ways to make her uncomfortable.

Oh, get a grip, Lily, she reprimanded herself silently. She was getting paranoid, and with no proof of any misdoing. If she didn't stop, she'd be seeing phantoms behind every tree.

The only real phantom was Kevin, sliding in and out of mirrors and sneaking up on people. But he'd come clean, and she needed to let it go. If she didn't, she was going to go crazy, and worse yet would be the indignity of being a certified lunatic.

She chuckled at the wholesome picture of being taken off in a straitjacket.

"Care to share the joke?" Kevin teased, nudging her with his shoulder.

"Oh, no," Lily said emphatically. "This is one joke I intend to keep to myself."

Chapter Twelve

Mack knew Lily suspected him of conspiring against her, and he couldn't keep the smile from his face no matter how hard he tried.

If she only knew the truth.

That her mother, the rich, esteemed old Adora Montague, would conspire against her for the good of true love was almost more than any man should have the privilege of knowing.

Of course, he wouldn't have known had he not been eavesdropping. But that aside, if anyone had plans today, it was Abby. She was fairly shaking with anticipation.

It could very well be she was close to a breakthrough, but he thought it was something entirely different making her so antsy and excited.

And he didn't want to know what.

"I'll put you up here, Abby," he instructed when they

reached the parallel bars. "I'm not going to let you go unless you say so. Don't worry about falling down. Even if I take my hands from you, I'll always catch you if your legs give out. Do you trust me?"

Abby laughed and nodded. "I've been doing lots of exercises on my legs."

"I know you have," he said, his voice thickening with pride. As far as he was concerned, this was his little girl, and she was a trooper. He could never tell her how much he admired her spirit and appreciated her inherent trust in him.

"Where do you want me?" Lily said. "Just tell me what to do and I'll do it."

"Why, you're her motivation, of course," he explained, reaching out to tip her playfully under the chin with his fingertip. "You get to be on the other end of the bars, holding your arms out to her. That will help her focus, and if God is willing, it will get her to the end of the line and into your arms on the first try."

"Okay," Lily said slowly. "I can do that."

He could hear the hesitation in her voice. She was wondering how much motivation she could be.

Didn't she realize he'd climb high mountain peaks and swim wide oceans if it meant her arms were open to him at the end of the trail?

Abby was no different. Her mother's love was the most motivating influence in her life, and it was the main reason she was getting better.

If only Lily could see it.

He chalked Abby's hands, placed her up on the rods and instructed her how to balance herself. "I've got your waist," he said reassuringly when she teetered. "Now don't be discouraged if you don't get very far time. Anything worth doing takes time. Just do what you can, and let me know when you get tired."

Abby was now completely concentrating on her limbs, her mouth pinched and her arms shaking with effort. Mack braced her small waist, using his thumbs on her spine to help steady her.

Lily reached out her hands. "Get your balance first, hon, before you try to move forward too much. I'm right here for you."

"I...know...Mom." Abby was already breathing heavily, and the strain showed on her face.

"Are you sure about this, kiddo?" Kevin asked, his heart wrenching for the pain she must be experiencing, both physically and emotionally. "We can wait until another time if you want."

"Of course she's sure," said a crackly old voice from behind him.

Adora. When had she come into the room?

"She knows what needs to be done," Adora said calmly, tapping her cane multiple times on the floor. "Get to it, Abigail."

"Mama!" Lily exclaimed. "Really. It's bad enough

that you—" she broke off suddenly, her face bright with the flush of anger. "Don't you go pushing Abigail. I won't let you."

"I don't think that's what your mother meant," Kevin broke in, trying to still the situation before it blew up completely.

"I know exactly what she meant," Lily said through gritted teeth.

"Hello…" Abigail reminded them from where she was suspended.

Mack met Lily's gaze and they both colored.

"Sorry, love," Mack apologized.

"We're ready," Lily assured her daughter. "You just let us know what you want to do."

"I want to walk across this thing," said Abigail, sounding at once agonized and eager.

"Let's do it," Mack encouraged.

Abigail took a slow, wobbly step that was more a turn of hip than leg movement. But it was movement, and Mack was overjoyed.

"Yes!" he exclaimed brightly. "Way to go, little girl."

"Can you make another step, honey?" Lily asked tentatively. Her arms were still reaching, coaxing, loving. Mack knew she would gladly take her daughter's place if she were able.

As would he.

He felt Abby tense for another step, but she surprised him—everyone—by taking three.

"Wow!" complimented Lily. "Look at you go. I had no idea."

With that praise, Abby made another three steps before resting again. She was using her legs now, though tentatively.

"You're going to have those braces off your legs before you know it, kid," Mack said.

With a sudden burst of energy, Abigail made another three steps, and then walked off the bars right into Lily's arms.

Lily was crying. Abigail was crying. And Mack, to his astonishment, felt tears wetting his own cheek.

He wanted to hug Abigail until she squealed, and kiss Lily good and hard, but this was a family moment, and he wasn't family. He stood up, backed up a few paces, placed his hands behind his back and waited.

"Kevin?" Abby reached out a hand for him. Lily's grateful brown eyes beckoned him as well.

That was all the invitation he needed. With a whoop he rushed forward, embracing them both and turning them around and around again until they were both laughing and squealing.

"My girls have had quite a day," he said, smiling from one to the other. "I'm so incredibly proud of you, Abby. You're such a strong young lady. You are the spitting image of your mother inside."

"Yes," agreed Adora, appearing before them with a

wheelchair. "And this strong young lady needs to rest now. Come along, Abigail, and I'll get you ready for a nap."

Mack knew Abby hated taking naps, but this once she didn't argue. He didn't know whether it was because she was genuinely fatigued after her monumental accomplishment, or because of the secret conspiracy he knew was loose in this cabin.

He tended toward his second opinion when Abby slipped from between them, not-so-subtly pulling his arm around Lily's waist. Not that he was about to argue with her efforts, not as long as Lily didn't notice or didn't care.

He didn't get to hold her in his arms nearly as much as he wanted to, which was all of the time, come to think of it. He would definitely have to stick with Abby's plan, whatever that was.

Lily looked up into Kevin's eyes and balked at the hazy, thoughtful look his expression conveyed. Suddenly she realized, as Adora closed the door to Abigail's bedroom, this quiet, reflective moment wasn't about the child anymore.

It was she and Kevin in a fire-blazing cabin with a new snowstorm starting outside that would no doubt blanket the hearty wildflowers like those Kevin and Abby had picked for her. Even now those flowers were on the sideboard scenting the entire cabin.

It was romantic.

How it had become that way eluded her, but panic rushed through her nonetheless. Suddenly his hand on her back felt as if it burned through her every bit as much as his gaze did.

She quickly stepped away from Kevin and started talking about the first thing to come to her mind. Besides romance, that is. "That was a significant breakthrough, wasn't it?"

"It was. She will recover quickly from here. She has a lot of fight and spirit in her. Your daughter is going to be running and playing with other children in no time, Lily."

She choked back a happy sob. "I'm so glad to hear it. You've done so much to help her."

Kevin shook his head. "Not me. You motivate her more than anyone. And she's got your spirit."

He underestimated himself. "You must know how much Abigail adores you."

He cleared his throat and looked away from her. "I return the sentiment," he said at last, turning his gaze back to her so she could tell how much he really meant what he said.

How had they gotten back on such a shaky foundation? She was trying to get away from this very thing, the look in his eyes that said he wasn't finished speaking and definitely not finished acting on those unspoken words lying like a gulf between them.

She didn't even want to know. She didn't want to hear

it. Her heart was in such turmoil she was about to spon-taneously combust.

Oh, *why* couldn't Kevin have been a nurse?

Why did he have to be a special agent? Why did he have to be the kind of man who carried a gun?

Why did she have to be the type of woman to be at-tracted to that type of man? Why did she have to be a woman who was genuinely terrified of guns? In Kevin she'd found all the things she had promised herself she would avoid at any cost.

Except it *did* matter.

She couldn't risk her own heart, and she certainly couldn't risk Abigail's.

"I think," Kevin said, "Abigail may have an emo-tional breakthrough soon, as well."

And then he was leaving.

That's what he was telling her. She was right to try to have guarded her heart, however miserably she had failed in the attempt.

"I see."

Kevin stepped forward and took her hands, and though she made a token resistance to the measure, he held them fast.

It was no use fighting the inevitable. He was stronger than she was, and though his touch was gentle, she knew he could be stubborn when he wanted to be.

Now being a perfect case in point.

She relaxed her stance and allowed him to hold her

hands, uncomfortable being face to face and still more uncomfortable with the soft, gentle stroking caress he was applying to the backs of her hands with his thumbs.

And his smile—that winsome smile of his that never ceased to make her heart beat double time.

"I know what you think you see, Lily, but you couldn't be more wrong," he said at last, his voice guttural, almost sounding like a growl. "Why can't you trust me? Abigail does."

"Abigail is a child," she snapped. "I've been around. I know better."

"You've been hurt," he conceded, his voice warm, deep, and rich. "But you're a brave woman, the bravest I've ever known. If you want to, you can risk it. You can give it another go."

"That's just it. I can't." She paused and tried to swallow. "I won't."

She felt him stiffen for a moment, but it didn't show on his face or in his green eyes, which stayed locked with hers, his feelings evident.

She didn't want to hurt him. She was in enough pain for both of them. The feelings she had for him were— confused. Unstable. She couldn't trust them and never would. But she didn't want to hurt him by being callous or brushing him off.

She opened her mouth to say so when he laid his index finger over her lips. "Don't speak," he said, his bass voice taking on new proportions. "Just listen."

She nodded, her heart pounding so hard she thought Kevin might be able to hear it.

"That afternoon when I told you I loved you, I didn't say it to scare you."

She opened her mouth again, but he shook his head with a half smile.

"I know you're not ready for a commitment, and I'm not asking for one," he continued.

She had just released her breath when he modified his sentence.

"Yet."

He moved his hands to the sides of her face, gently cupping her jaw with his calloused palms. "You are so beautiful. Your skin is so soft," he whispered into her ear.

"Kevin, I—" she started, but once again he cut her off before she could speak.

"Listen to me, Lily Montague. I may not be asking for a commitment at this moment, but I don't want you to have any doubt as to my feelings for you. I love you, and I want to spend the rest of my life proving that. I also happen to be crazy in love with that little girl of yours."

Lily nodded slightly, keenly aware of the tips of his fingers at her jawline. "I know you are," she whispered.

Which was all the more reason she should be running out of this room at full speed, even if it was straight into a snowstorm.

But she couldn't move. She couldn't breathe. She

could only lift her chin and stare at Kevin. His gaze was fiercely intense, and there was no doubt in Lily's mind he believed what he said.

She had to talk him out of it. She had to make him understand why guns and special agents could not be a part of her and Abigail's lives. Especially after what her daughter had been through.

"There is nobody else on this planet for my heart except for you, Lily. You're the one. And when you are ready, with God's help, I will find you. Do you understand what I'm telling you?"

His last words were said in such a tight, scratchy voice that Lily knew the man in all his gallantry was pulling back with all his might, restraining what he really wanted to say.

And what *she* really wanted to say had to remain hidden in her heart forever.

His eyes blazing, he put the slightest pressure on her jaw, tenderly drawing her to him. His gaze was locked with hers, his smile as intense as his eyes.

She knew she shouldn't do this. It was a mistake to lead him on in any way, and it wasn't fair to him, either. She should it break off now and walk away.

But what harm would one last kiss do? She sensed with every fiber of her being that he was going away soon, and this would be all she would have to remember him by.

She didn't need any reminder of what it felt like to be alone.

She tried to pull away, for Kevin's sake, but she couldn't move a muscle. For the first time in her life, her heart was in control.

Kevin winged butterfly kisses over her lips, her cheek, her forehead, her eyes.

When his lips once more covered hers, it was a light and gentle touch, the sweet caress of the Kevin she knew and...*loved.*

Suddenly he deepened the kiss, fiercely proving to her both his love and his intentions. It was a desperate kiss, a kiss that forcefully begged a response.

She couldn't help but oblige. Her arms of their own accord wrapped around his neck as he dropped his hands to her waist and pulled her closer.

She needed this moment more than she had realized. She needed to spend this precious little time with him before it was too late.

Her hands explored the muscular planes of his shoulders, and then she stiffened when her fingers encountered the thick leather straps of his shoulder holster.

Suddenly, she knew exactly what was happening, and a combination of anger, sorrow and denial rushed through her, making her head spin with the knowledge and the emotional knife thrust into her gut.

He was kissing her goodbye.

Chapter Thirteen

Mack couldn't sleep.

It had been nearly a week since Abby started walking, and his instincts told him a major breakthrough was waiting right around the corner.

It was the wait that was killing him. He had even resorted to a glass of warm milk, but even that did not calm his nerves.

Lily had barely spoken to him since that afternoon. It was as if he was already gone.

She would never understand the reasons he had to go. Yes, there was the boy, the senator's son. But it was more than that.

It was honor. And integrity.

This was his job, had been his entire life until he met Lily. Now, *she* was everything to him. Even so, he had to finish what he started.

He had to leave.

What she didn't understand was that he would be back. He would follow her to the ends of the earth. He had to be with her.

He knelt by the bed, clasping his hands hard on his forehead.

"Lord give me strength," he whispered hoarsely. *"I need wisdom. Help me know what to do."*

His heart was aching so hard he thought a heart attack might be less painful. He stayed on his knees, not speaking, but silently communing with his Lord. Jesus might not be talking audibly, but he felt the presence of God rushing over him, taking his fear and washing it as far away from him as the depths of the ocean.

Finally, after a time, he felt calm and once more in control. Not in control, really. God had that one covered.

But what Mack could do, he would do.

And somehow, he would be with Lily in the end. He had to be.

Suddenly there was a sharp shriek, and Mack jumped to his feet and reached for his gun. Slowly, carefully, he opened his door and slid silently down the hallway. His heart was in his throat and pounding wildly.

The scream had come from Abby's room.

The door was half open, so he pointed his gun and crashed through, quickly taking stock of the situation, the number of people and what was going on.

Adora and Lily sat on opposite sides of Abby's bed, comforting her with soft words.

There was no need for a gun, but there was a clear need for his presence. Since he hadn't been wearing a holster, he tucked his pistol in the back of his jeans and moved to sit on the edge of the bed next to Lily, leaning over Abby.

"What happened?" he asked, reaching out to straighten a lock of Abby's golden hair with his finger. "Are you okay, love?"

Abby nodded, but she looked as if she had seen a ghost. Her face was as white as a sheet and her eyes were wide with fright.

"She had a nightmare," Lily whispered softly, keeping her arms firmly around the small girl. "A bad nightmare. But she's awake now, and everything will be okay. Isn't that right, honey?"

Abby's eyes widened even further as she reached out to Mack, shaking her head wildly at her mother's gentle suggestion.

Adora didn't say a word. She sat prim and stiff-backed on the other edge of the bed with one hand softly stroking Abby's back.

Mack took Abby's small hands in his own. "What is it, love? Do you want to talk about it?"

She nodded as voraciously as she had shaken her head moments before.

"What is it, honey?" Lily asked, sounding stunned and worried.

Mack shot Lily a reassuring look, then turned his gaze back upon Abby.

"Anytime you're ready, love. We're all here for you—your mom, *Grand-mère* and me. And you know we'll protect you, right?"

A tear slid down the girl's face and her gaze dropped to where Mack held her hands. "I remember."

Adrenaline rushed through Mack, but he strove not to have it show either on his expression or in his grip. He was here for Abby first. Any information he got for the case was secondary.

"I was playing with Jeremy on the playground," she said hesitantly. It was obvious it was taking every bit of her courage to say the words.

"Go on," he whispered.

"Three people with guns came running in, yelling and scaring all the kids. Everyone started screaming and running.

"I didn't know what to do, so I just stood there. Jeremy tried to pull me toward the school, but I was afraid, and I couldn't move."

She stopped then and gulped air into her lungs. Kevin ran a hand over her hair and murmured words of encouragement, telling her she could take her time, and she didn't have to continue if she didn't want to.

But Abby was determined, and Mack was awed by her courage. "There were three bad guys running around the playground screaming at the kids. I thought they must be looking for somebody.

"Then someone pushed me aside and grabbed Jeremy." She stopped again and squeezed Mack's hands hard. "He was screaming. I tried to hold on to his hand, but—"

She stopped then and looked at her lap, tears pouring silently down her face. No one said a word; they just sat with her, exchanging worried glances amongst themselves at the little girl's plight.

"I couldn't help him, Kevin," she said with a sob and a hiccup.

"No one expected you to, love," Mack said hurriedly. "These were professional bad guys. Even the FBI is having trouble getting them. Don't feel bad."

It didn't seem enough to reassure her, but she went on talking.

"I saw that bad person turn around with Jeremy screaming and kicking in their arms. And then I got ran over, and I don't remember any more after that."

"You've done well, sweetheart," Lily encouraged, giving her daughter a squeeze. "And now that you've told us about it, I don't think you'll have as many bad dreams anymore."

"That's right," Mack added. "You're going to be all better now."

"What about Jeremy?"

Complete silence enveloped the room.

"We're doing everything we can to get him back

home safely," Mack said, clenching his teeth. He didn't want to do this, but he had to. He only hoped the two women in the room would understand. "If you feel up to it, kiddo, you might be able to help us rescue Jeremy."

Abby wrinkled her brow. "How, Kevin? I want to help Jeremy."

"I know you do, love. I'll tell you what. I want you to close your eyes. Remember, *Grand-mère* and your mom are right here with you. So am I. You're surrounded by people who love you."

Abby nodded and closed her eyes.

"Okay, now, I want you to forget everything that happened to you that day. Forget all the details around you. I just want you to concentrate on the fellow who grabbed Jeremy. Think hard, Abby. Do you remember anything about him? What he looked like?"

"But they were all wearing ski masks," she said, shaking her head and frowning in concentration. "They were all dressed in black, with black jackets and black boots and gloves."

"What kind of boots?" Kevin asked gently.

"I don't know. Like yours, I guess."

"Military boots?"

She shrugged. "Maybe."

"Okay. That helps a lot." It wasn't information he could use, but he didn't tell Abby. Military boots could be bought at outlet stores.

"Anything else, kiddo?"

Abby squeezed her eyes tightly closed for a minute, clearly straining to remember.

"It's okay, love. Don't pressure yourself," he advised, squeezing her hands. "We've probably done enough for one day."

"Wait!" she shrieked, sitting straight up. "I remember!"

"What, honey?" Lily asked excitedly. "Tell us what you remember."

"When Jeremy was fighting to get away, he grabbed a glove loose."

"And?" Mack prompted.

"The hand. Kevin, it was a woman's hand."

"What?" He tried not to shout. "Are you sure about that, Abby?"

"Yes. Before she ran me over, I looked at her. Once I'd seen her hand, I could tell she was a woman."

"Abby, I can't tell you how good you've been to us today. This might be exactly the information we need to break the case." Mack couldn't keep the excitement out of his voice.

"And rescue Jeremy?" she asked.

"I'm going to do my very best. I promise." He choked up on the words.

He stayed with the girl for a few more minutes, his mind sifting through the information, figuring out various scenarios possible now that they knew the perpetrator was a woman.

What kind of woman would steal a small boy and

knock over and paralyze a little girl? What possible motive could she have for such things?

He needed to pack his bag and get back to headquarters as fast as possible. Too much time had gone by already. The possibility of finding Jeremy alive went down with every minute he wasted.

He hated what he had to do—hated it with every fiber of his being.

It was time to leave.

Lily knew the moment Abby had the breakthrough that Kevin would be leaving. He hadn't said anything, just hurriedly returned to his room and closed the door, his brow creased.

But she knew.

And despite her best efforts to protect herself from this moment, her heart was breaking.

She poked the fire in the great room and sat down on the sofa, leaning her head back with a soft sigh. She felt cold, though the fire was blazing in the hearth and she had a warm bathrobe wrapped around her in addition to her sweats.

She'd known this day would come ever since the moment Kevin had stepped out of the bushes of her mother's garden with a gun in his hand.

So why did it still hurt so much?

She knew the answer to that question, even if she was adamantly unwilling to admit it, even to herself. There was a perfect explanation for why she didn't want to see him go.

She was in love with him.

Despite the fact that he carried a gun. Despite the fact he was an FBI special agent.

Love had its own song, and it was a tune Lily was no longer familiar with. Would she sacrifice everything she'd learned over the years to be with him?

She knew the answer to that question, too.

But the answers had come too late. She would not barge in on Kevin now, not when he was busy preparing to leave with critical information that might save little Jeremy McCain's life. He must not be distracted from the work he had to do, not even for love.

Had she realized earlier what her heart had known all along, they might have made plans together, decided what to do when all was said and done. They could have made plans for the future.

But she'd been foolish. And silent.

Now, there was no future.

Mack exploded from the bedroom in a rush of activity. His single bag was packed and dangling from his shoulder. He was wearing khaki pants, a dress shirt and a tie. She'd never seen him dressed in anything but jeans, and she almost thought she liked the jeans better. Kevin was not the kind of man made to wear a suit and tie.

Obviously he was going straight to FBI headquarters in Denver without delay. She'd at least thought he would spend the night, as it was already well past two o'clock in the morning.

"Lily," he said, clearly surprised she was there. "I didn't expect you to be awake."

"Obviously." Her gaze traveled to his bag. "Sneaking out in the middle of the night, are we?"

It was an accusation, and he clearly knew it. He colored under her indicting gaze, and she knew she'd guessed right.

"Ah," he said, clearing his throat. "In all the excitement, I didn't really think about it. I guess I was worried about getting to headquarters."

"And what do you suppose Abigail would think about that?"

He blanched. "I wouldn't intentionally hurt anyone. I thought it would be best to get on the road as soon as possible."

"Yes, of course you're right," she agreed, feeling as if a dagger had pierced her heart.

She knew the truth. He wasn't hurrying to headquarters. He'd been trying to get away without having to see *her*.

To flee without so much as a goodbye.

Well, he was stuck now. He was going to have to confront her, and *she* was going to confront him. She wasn't going to let him leave without telling him how she felt.

She was working up the nerve to speak when Adora scuffled down the hall in her bathrobe and fluffy pink slippers, her gray hair in curlers that looked a little askew from sleeping on them.

"So you're going, then," Adora said as a given statement. "God's best to you, young man."

"Thank you, ma'am," Kevin said, moving to shake her hand. "Do you think it would be okay for me to wake up Abby to say goodbye?"

"That's up to Lily, but I'm sure that wouldn't be a problem. Abby would want to say goodbye to you."

Mack slid his glance to Lily. "Well?"

"Of course we should wake up Abigail," she said. "She would be devastated if you left without telling her goodbye."

Lily was talking about herself more than Abigail, but Kevin didn't have to know.

She followed him into Abigail's room and watched as he sat on the side of the bed and gently stroked the child's hair. He didn't wake her immediately, but sat staring at her with his wide green eyes full of emotion. She watched him swallow hard, and suspected he was holding back a tear or two.

He really did love Abigail.

At length he took the child's arm and gently shook her awake. She immediately put her arms around Kevin's neck and hugged him hard.

"You're leaving," she stated, every bit as emphatic as Adora had been.

"Yes, kiddo, I'm afraid so," Kevin choked out, stroking the girl's hair. "I want to stay here with you, but I have a job to do."

Abigail nodded soberly. "Rescue Jeremy."

"Just so. I promise I will do everything in my power to find your friend and get him back home safe where he belongs."

"You will," Abigail said confidently.

"You can help," he said, setting her back down on the bed and gently tucking her in.

"What?"

"You can pray. Every night when your mother tucks you in, you can remember to say a prayer for Jeremy. We might not know where he is right now, but God does. And God can keep him safe and bring him home."

"I promise," Abigail said softly.

"I promise, too," said Lily, tears in her eyes. "I'll pray for little Jeremy. And I'll pray for you, too, Kevin."

The tender, agonized look he gave her almost sent her into a fit of sobbing. She wished she'd kept her mouth shut.

With a tender kiss on Abigail's cheek, he made sure she was tucked in well and smiled tightly as he said his last goodbye.

When they were in the hallway, Adora cleared her throat loudly. "Well, I'm headed off to bed. It's ridiculous to be up at this time of night."

"Goodnight, then," Kevin said, laying a hand on the old woman's shoulder. "Sleep well."

"God be with you, son," Adora said, her voice unusually husky. It was the most emotion Lily had ever heard in her mother's voice. It choked Lily up even more.

"And with you," Kevin replied. He placed a tentative kiss on Adora's cheek, which she surprisingly accepted with grace. Then she turned away and walked sedately back to her bedroom, dignified even in curlers and fuzzy pink slippers.

"I guess it's just the two of us," Kevin said, taking Lily's arm and leading her back into the great room. Then he surprised her by saying in a low, gruff voice full of emotion, "Thank you."

"For what?" she asked, equally affected.

"For stopping me from leaving tonight. I was taking the coward's way out. I needed to talk to everyone." He paused. "Especially you."

"Why?"

"Because I have a lot to say to you. Things you need to know."

So it was work-related. Lily shouldn't have been surprised, but she was.

"Let me know what I need to do. I want to help you, to do everything in my power to help save Jeremy from this vicious woman."

He turned and took her hands. "I'm not talking about Jeremy." His gaze bored into hers, asking questions to which she didn't have answers, or at least, answers she could formulate into words.

"What, then?" she croaked.

"I love you, Lily, and I always will. I have to go away right now, but I will come back. I will find you. Maybe then we will be able to plan a future together. Maybe then—"

He cut it short, but Lily knew what he was going to say. Maybe then she would have worked out her problems and be able to commit.

This was it. This was the moment she'd been praying for. This was when she declared her feelings so Kevin knew he would come back to requited love.

She opened her mouth, but nothing came out.

She had rehearsed this moment a hundred times, but she had so many things to tell him they got garbled in her mind and did not make it to her tongue.

"I promise I'll find you," said Kevin huskily, and then quickly cupped her jaw in one hand and kissed her hard.

A moment later he had grasped for his bag and was out the door, leaving Lily standing mute and wounded.

The door of opportunity had just slammed in her face.

Chapter Fourteen

The first week, Lily jumped at every knock and telephone call. Her mind was always on Kevin, and she held her breath for his promised return.

She hadn't heard a word from him since he'd left. At least he might have called to say he was okay, but that call never came.

Then again, why should he call her?

She hadn't given him any reason to return. When she should have spoken up, she'd been densely silent. Who could blame the man if he didn't want to speak to her ever again?

God had given her the chance at a new beginning. He was the One in control of living and dying, of little boys being rescued from kidnappers without a scratch and of crippled little girls walking again. Every moment of life was a precious gift—a miracle. Hadn't almost losing Abigail taught her anything?

Why hadn't she said anything to Kevin when she had the chance? Why hadn't she given him a glimpse of her true heart?

She suspected she would have a lifetime to regret it.

Kevin was gone. And as each day went by, it looked more and more as if he wasn't going to return.

She considered the idea of hunting him down, but quickly shuffled that thought from her mind. After all, why would he want to see her now? If he didn't come for her, he must have a good reason—he must not want to see her again.

He was done with his shift of tolerating the bitter widow of Montague Mansion. He was no doubt rejoicing at his narrow escape.

She knew she sounded nasty and coldhearted, but she wasn't. Not really.

She was heartbroken.

And yet she hoped.

The second week, word was given through a special agent—not Kevin—that the case had been solved and Jeremy had been reunited with his family.

With this news came the welcome information that it was safe to return to the Montague Mansion. So they packed up their belongings and were escorted to the only place Lily could call home at the moment. Abigail was walking somewhat steadily now, her strength improving every day. That was a blessing.

Still, Kevin didn't call or return. Lily thought he

should at least call to let them know the details of how the job had gone down.

He had been there when the woman holding Jeremy had been taken down, this much she knew. Surely he had to know they would want to hear every detail.

From him.

Of course, she already knew most of what had happened from speaking with various agents and reading the many newspaper articles on the subject. But she didn't want the newspaper account.

She wanted the man with the wavy dark-brown hair, hooded big green eyes and heart-stopping half smile to tell her. To be here with her.

She had been the one to explain the story to Abigail and Adora. Once the FBI knew the primary suspect was a woman, Kevin and the other agents went right to work, interviewing the senator and following leads.

Senator McCain was heading up the committee on a bill regarding the sentences of child kidnappers. The woman they arrested, Maribell Adams, had been nagging the senator nonstop to make the bill more stringent. Her own daughter had been kidnapped, and the outcome hadn't been as happy as that of Jeremy.

The little girl had been murdered.

Finally, the woman, in a haze of fury, decided to hire some criminal types to help her kidnap the senator's son. She thought, in her grieved irrationality, that if the senator himself experienced the keen terror of losing his own son, he would then be more open to her point of view.

Jeremy had been treated like royalty. Maribell had no intention of hurting the little boy—she only wanted to make a point. So he had slept in a soft feather bed, had had plenty of good, nutritious food and all the video games he wanted to play.

When they arrested her, they found Jeremy in fine shape and only a little frightened at being taken away from his parents.

As far as what Maribell had inadvertently done to Abigail, she displayed genuine remorse and wrote a letter to apologize for the tragedy.

Lily thought the woman would probably do some time in a mental institution until she could work out her issues and get a better grasp on reality.

Maribell wasn't her biggest concern.

The crisis was over, and other than filing paperwork, she couldn't imagine why Kevin didn't come. She watched the road constantly, then berated herself for doing so.

It was time for her to face the truth.

Kevin wasn't coming back.

Her whole being was filled with a sense of emptiness and loss, but she knew facing the truth was for the best. It was time for her to return to Washington, D.C., and go back to work. It was time to give Abigail a normal life again.

But she didn't pack, and she didn't leave. She supposed she, too, needed time to heal. She prayed God would release her from the horrible ache, and though it still hurt, she found it a little more bearable by focusing on all the good God had done in her life.

And then came the invitation, by special courier, a large, square white envelope written in calligraphy and sealed with red wax.

It had Lily's name on it, and for a brief, fleeting moment she thought it might be one of Kevin's crazy escapades. He had done worse.

Her heart raced as she broke the seal, and then dropped into her stomach when she pulled out the invitation. It wasn't from Kevin at all.

It was from Senator McCain. He was holding a fancy ball to celebrate his son's homecoming. He wanted Lily and Abigail to come a week from Tuesday. It was Monday, giving them a week and a day to decide.

The senator wanted to honor Abigail, too, so Lily didn't see how she could gracefully bow out, even though she had no desire whatsoever to go to any sort of public function, much less a fancy ball.

She didn't want to dress up, put her hair up and makeup on her face. She didn't want to talk about nothing to people she didn't know.

But she knew she would accept, because this night would be important to Abigail, and the little girl deserved to be recognized for all she had been through.

Lily would have to put a pretty face on it, even if she was gritting her teeth on the inside.

When she told Abigail about the invitation, the girl shrieked with excitement. She would get to wear a pretty dress and shiny shoes, better than those she wore for church every Sunday.

Lily assured her they would find the perfect dress for her, and that she would be the prettiest lady at the reception. Shoes, bows, they would go for everything.

She didn't want to buy anything for herself, but Abigail insisted, and, in addition to Abigail's pink satin, she found herself buying a white lace gown that, in retrospect, reminded her far too much of a wedding dress.

With all they had to do, their flight to Washington, D.C., came far too fast for Lily. And as she and her daughter dressed for the ball in the hotel room she'd rented, she really began having doubts.

How would she make it through this night? She'd be under rapt observation as Abigail's mother, when all she really wanted to do was crawl into the nearest hole and hide.

But Lily had never been one to run from her problems, and this wasn't going to be a first. Gathering all her courage, she said a silent prayer for strength and followed Abigail down the hotel hallway and outside, where a black stretch limousine ordered by Senator McCain waited to transport them to the reception.

The senator had rented a gorgeous old Victorian mansion that had been converted to a reception hall. He had gone to every length to dress up the place, from rolling out red carpet on the stairs to the winter pine wreaths decorating the walls.

The lighting was low and flickering with many candles lining every wall, giving the room an enchanted effect. Even Lily pulled in her breath when she saw it. Hors d'oeuvres waited in every corner, along with green-colored punch and water.

There were an incredible number of people milling about the room, and Lily felt a moment of claustrophobia. She took a deep breath. She would get through it. She always did. For Abigail's sake, if for no other reason. She must do this for her daughter, even if she herself didn't want to be around people.

Abigail, in her pink satin, was clinging to Lily's hand as they walked into the midst of the crowd. Lily gave her hand a squeeze for reassurance. She'd been thinking so much of herself, she hadn't considered how her poor daughter must be feeling.

She leaned down to the child's level. "This is all for you, you know."

The child's eyes were gleaming. "Not *just* for me, Mommy," she said, breaking into the biggest smile Lily had seen in months.

Lily assumed Abigail was referring to Jeremy, so she didn't question the odd statement further. She was glad the girl was so excited about the happy return of her classmate and friend.

She heard an orchestra tuning up, but couldn't locate it through the crowd. She'd known a black-tie affair such as this one would have live music, but still gave her a shiver. She had avoided listening to anything remotely close to romantic music because it brought her feelings too close to the surface.

She was here, and she would support Abigail with every fiber of her being, even if every song the orchestra played rent her heart anew. But in the end, she decided she didn't really need to worry about it. She was merely making up scenarios in her mind that put additional stress on her.

Why was she doing that? She already had more than enough problems to deal with in reality, thank you very much. A little music couldn't hurt her.

The tinkling of a spoon on glass turned everyone's attention to a raised platform on the far side of the room, where Senator McCain stood before a microphone, looking very much as if he intended to make a speech.

Lily pulled Abigail closer to her and wove her way around the muddle of people until they stood near the front. She wanted to make sure Abigail heard all the good things the senator was bound to say about her.

The senator leaned forward toward the mike. "Is this thing on?" he called loudly, sending a high-pitched feedback through the air. He laughed and took a step backwards.

Senator McCain was an older, balding man in his mid-fifties who looked as if he'd had a great deal too much of his charming wife's home cooking. With his glistening round face and pink cheeks, he looked as if he'd just come in from the snow, but Lily knew the truth—it was little Jeremy at his side that had the senator beaming with joy.

"Please. Everyone get yourself a cup of our good green punch. I would like to make a couple of toasts."

The crowd began swarming again, with so many voices buzzing Lily couldn't tell them apart. Though she'd worked in D.C. for years, crowds always made her head spin, and tonight was no exception. Still, they needed punch, for she was positive the senator would call Abigail forward during his toast.

"Stay here and save our place near the front," she said in Abigail's ear, a little louder than a whisper so she could be heard above the noise. She waved at Senator McCain and gestured at him to keep an eye on Abigail.

If she could fight her way through the crowds, she thought with a grimace. She highly doubted it.

She saw many familiar faces and was greeted often on her trek to the punch table. It took her forever to make her way around, and she worried about Abigail, standing all by herself with so many people around.

Still, she appreciated the kind wishes from work acquaintances who knew her daughter's story. Apparently, many prayers had been said on Abigail's behalf, and for that she was thankful.

Senator McCain started his speech before she could return to Abigail with the two punch glasses. He related the story of his son's disappearance to the fascinated crowd, how Jeremy was plucked up from the playground and taken away by a woman driven mad by her own daughter's disappearance and violent death.

He thanked God publicly that the boy had been returned safely from the terrifying weeks of his captivity, and he promised he would continue working on the bill that would bring about harsher punishments for kidnappers.

At the same time, he expressed regret and sorrow for the state of Maribell Adams, his son's kidnapper. Lily was impressed by the senator's humble heart and his ability to see beyond his anger and show compassion. She herself had had a harder time finding it in her heart to forgive Mrs. Adams for paralysing Abigail.

The senator's words gave her pause. What would she do if she had lost Abigail? Perhaps she, too, would have gone crazy with grief.

Closing her eyes, she offered up a prayer, first of forgiveness for her own angry heart, and then of forgiveness for Maribell Adams for her actions which had so disrupted their family.

When she was finished, her heart was lightened and her mood improved. She almost felt like singing.

Almost.

"I hope…" the senator said, choking up a bit, "I hope I've become a better father through the course of this terrible ordeal. As you all know, I have a difficult career when it comes to family issues. But as of today, my very first priorities are my wife and son. If I'm missing in action on the Hill, you'll know right where to find me—out fishing with Jeremy."

The crowd laughed and clapped for the ruddy-faced senator.

"I hope everyone will learn from my experience," he said, suddenly grave. "Don't overlook your loved ones in your hurry to get through life. If you find true love, grab for it with all your heart. I'm so blessed with Sarah, my own wife of sixteen years."

Again he had to stop due to the applause he received at his statement.

As soon as he had said the words, Lily was overwhelmed with memories of Kevin—their indoor picnic, the gazebo, his protection of her, the horseback riding, the wildflowers.

She felt like choking, for her lungs had ceased to work. Why couldn't she have seen the truth when Kevin was there beside her? That he wasn't here now was entirely her fault.

She wished she had it all to do over again, especially those last few moments when she could have told Kevin what was truly in her heart. But she probably would have been just as obtuse and stubborn a second time through, so maybe things were just as well left as they were.

"And if God has blessed you with a son or daughter," the senator continued, swinging into political speech mode, "don't ever take that for granted. Give that child a hug and kiss each and every day, and be sure and tell them you love them. Don't just assume they know. Let them hear it out of your mouth every day of their young lives."

Lily swallowed hard at the senator's strong admonition. She might have ruined things with Kevin, but Abigail was standing right in front of her, her leg braces hidden underneath her long, frilly satin dress.

Looking at her little girl now, she realized how fast the years had gone by since Abigail was a baby, contented merely to rock in her mother's arms.

How far she'd come. She was growing up by the minute, and becoming more and more independent with each step she took.

Lily stopped herself and threw her arms around Abigail's neck. With a big, smacking kiss, she squeezed her daughter tight in her arms.

"Mom…Mom! You're squishing me," Abigail protested, wriggling out of her arms. "I don't think Senator McCain meant *right now*."

"And why not?" Lily argued, perching her hands on her hips. "I happen to love you very much, young lady, and I don't care who knows it."

Abigail sighed loudly and wiped a hand down her face, looking thoroughly put out. "I do."

Lily laughed. "If I promise not to accost you, will you hold my hand, at least?"

"I guess." Abigail offered her hand, and Lily took it, resisting the urge to squeeze.

"And so," concluded Senator McCain, "I make a toast to my son." He raised his punch glass.

The crowd followed. "To Jeremy!"

The poor boy looked at least as uncomfortable as Abigail did, with his father's arms around him and the crowd cheering him on. His face was flushed and he was squirming, pulling at his bow tie.

"And now," continued the senator, "I have another story to tell, one about the brave little girl who helped find my son."

"He's not going to make me go up there, is he?" Abigail whispered desperately.

"I'm afraid so, hon," Lily replied, using the moment to get in a good hand squeeze. "That's why we're here—to honor you."

"But I didn't do anything!" she protested. "All I did was get runned over."

"Everyone in this room knows how much courage it took for you to get yourself better so you could help Kevin and the other agents find Jeremy. Without your information, it never would have happened. You're a hero."

Abigail shrugged and shook her head. "Great. Just great."

Lily laughed.

The senator finished a short rendition of what had happened to Abigail that tragic day in the schoolyard, and how hard she had worked to recover.

"I am pleased to inform you all that Abby Montague is here tonight with us. And she's able to walk!"

The crowd roared with approval.

"Abby, do you want to come up here for a moment so we all can congratulate you?"

"No," Abigail muttered under her breath, but she put a smile on and stepped forward with a little nudge from Lily to get her going.

Fear of the spotlight aside, Abigail was a natural. She smiled and waved, and even lifted her skirt a bit so people could see the leg braces she still wore.

"Now if these were old-fashioned times where the father made the decisions on who his son would marry, you can bet these two cute kids would already be betrothed."

The crowd laughed at the faces the children made at the thought.

"See how far things have come in the world, ladies and gentlemen? Children make their own choices, and rightly so. But I suspect Jeremy and Abigail will be the best of friends for the rest of their lives. Tragedy bonds all people firmly together."

Abigail subtly widened her gaze at Lily, clearly asking for this to be finished before she fainted from embarrassment. The look on her face showed that this public appearance seemed worse to her than all the months of painful exercises she'd been through to get her legs working.

Lily took pity on her. She went to the podium and stepped up next to Abigail and lifted her glass. "To my daughter, Abigail."

"To Abigail," the crowd echoed, raising their glasses at the child.

"Thanks, Mom," whispered Abigail as they moved away into the crowd. "I didn't think he was ever going to stop talking."

"Believe me, if this wasn't entirely necessary we wouldn't be here."

"Oh, no, we had to be here tonight," Abigail said.

"Why?" Lily probed, more than a little curious. Her daughter obviously wasn't leaning toward a career in politics.

"Because—uh—because we had to toast Jeremy." Abigail didn't sound particularly sure of herself, though, and Lily continued to gaze at her daughter, trying to figure out what was really going on.

"Good. Now we can leave. What do you say we go get some ice cream and call it a night?"

"No!" Abigail was emphatic. Giving up the offer of ice cream? That definitely wasn't like her.

"You're sure you want to stay?" Lily asked.

"The party is just starting, Mom. It's going to get fun pretty soon, I know it is. It's better than being in that cabin!"

Lily's immediate reaction was to disagree, she hadn't felt alone in that cabin, and she certainly hadn't been lonely, not with Kevin there.

She was lonely *now*. She wanted to run out of this room and not look back.

But Abigail was seven. The flicker of the candles, the crowd, the hardwood floor and the strains of the live orchestra must seem like a fairy tale to the little girl.

So for Abigail's sake, she would stay, even if the flickering candles were giving her a headache instead of dreams come true. At least she would do what she could to make her daughter's night one she would never forget.

They found a couple of chairs up against one wall. Groups of elegant couples mingled in every corner of the room, the men in their dark formals and the ladies clad in shimmering gowns in every color of the rainbow.

Lily had to admit it really did look a bit like Cinderella's ball. Elegant and sophisticated. All the things Lily wasn't and didn't care to be.

Hadn't that been half the reason she'd left home at eighteen? She was glad she had reconciled with her mother at long last, even if they would never see eye-to-eye.

At least the orchestra appeared to have captured an

age gone by, playing soft, romantic big band music that was a perfect fit for the evening. Probably the worst choice for Lily's heart, however.

"Mom," Abigail said, sounding put out. "Mom, I've called you three times now."

Lily laughed. "Sorry. I was lost in thought, watching the beautiful dresses."

"Don't watch," her daughter said, standing up and holding her hand out to Lily. "Walk around with me. I'm tired of sitting down."

"Oh, Abby, honey, I really don't think—"

"Hey," her daughter interrupted. "You just called me *Abby*."

Lily frowned. "I did not."

"Did too. That's cool, Mom. I like it. That's what Kevin calls me."

Called, Lily corrected silently.

"Come on, Mom. I know you know a lot of these people. Talk to them."

Lily let herself be dragged to the nearest group of people, reminding herself that she was here for Abby—Abigail—and that she should take the senator's advice to heart.

It turned out she did know several people in the group, and she introduced her beaming daughter with more than a touch of pride.

"It's good to see you, Abby!" exclaimed Emily, a senator from North Carolina and a good friend of Lily's.

"Why don't you spin around for us, Abby, and show off your beautiful dress?"

Abby began whirling in circles. Round and round she flew, her flaxen hair tossing like strands of gold as she moved.

They might be short on Prince Charmings tonight, but her daughter was truly a princess.

"I've about had it," Lily told her smiling daughter later. "Your poor mother needs to go home and rest."

"Oh, not yet, Mom. Please." The orchestra struck up a slow ballad. "This is my favoritist song."

Lily raised an eyebrow. "Your favoritist song?" she repeated. "Honey, they haven't been playing anything more recent than the forties all night."

"Well, it's my favorite song now," Abby insisted. "I'll remember this song forever and ever."

When she put it that way, how could Lily refuse?

Abby whirled around again, clearly joyous about her ability to move.

"You're pretty tonight," announced Jeremy from behind Lily, looking dapper in his little tuxedo.

God really was good, all the time. She closed her eyes and prayed, thanking God for His blessings.

She opened them to find Abby looking at her with a pleading, if pointed, message she wanted her mother gone. *Now.*

As a mother, she didn't know exactly how she felt about that, but she knew when it was time to bow out gracefully.

"I, uh, see Senator Murphy over there," she said in croaking voice. "I really need to speak to him. Will you two be okay?"

Abby rolled her eyes.

It was so cute Lily wanted to laugh, and so unnerving she wanted to cry. She stood in the middle of the floor watching the children talk, obviously comfortable with each other, and it wasn't long before a number of other children their age joined the group.

Sighing under her breath, Lily supposed she should have that "talk" with the "Senator" and went outside to a small balcony for a breath of fresh air. A moment alone out of the din of the room wouldn't hurt. She leaned on the railing and studied the houses surrounding the old Victorian inn.

At first she didn't notice the gentle tap on her shoulder, as she was completely lost in thought. It was only when she was wheeled around did she know he wanted her attention.

Kevin.

Even in the moonlit darkness, she admired his black cutaway coat with a white shirt and black cravat. He looked like something out of the nineteenth century. His broad shoulders filled out the coat to perfection, and his gleaming green eyes completed the picture perfectly.

Her prince.

Without thinking, she threw herself at him, clamping her arms around his neck as he whirled her around and around, her feet flying well off the ground.

"I'm happy to see you, too, sweetheart," he said, laughing loudly.

"I didn't think you were coming back," she blurted into his ear. "I thought I'd never see you again, never be able to tell you."

He set her back down on her feet, but her head was still spinning.

Chapter Fifteen

Mack's head was spinning, too. He and Abby and even Adora had all conspired for this surprise, but now that he was here, he couldn't believe it was real, that Lily was back in his arms where she belonged.

He cupped her face gently, his fingertips lining her jaw. She smelled like the wildflowers he had picked her a month ago.

There, in the secluded darkness of the balcony, he kissed her with all his heart, until Lily could only cling to him. "I told you I'd come back."

She shook her head. "That first week—and then the second…" Her voice sounded gruff and uneven, as if she were choking.

He slid his arms more tightly around her waist in answer to her unspoken question. Lily looked almost shy as she slid her hands up to his shoulders.

"What was it you thought you'd never be able to tell me?" he asked, so close to her ear he could inhale the sweet scent of her perfume.

She met his gaze for a long moment.

"The day you left," she said at last, "you told me you loved me and would come back for me."

"And so I have."

"But I said nothing. I gave you no reason to return, no indication of my feelings at all."

"That's why I gave you time, why I didn't come back right away. So you could work things out and realize we needed to be together. You've been through so much. It's no wonder you're hesitant to believe what a man tells you."

"I've paid for that pause, Kevin—this time without you has been awful. I counted the minutes until you would return. And when you didn't—"

He kissed her to keep her from completing the sentence. "I have returned, just as I promised. I'm here now, and I'm not going to leave you ever again."

"I love you," Lily professed in a blur of words. "I should have told you the day you left. I wanted to tell you, ached to tell you, but the words wouldn't come."

"Lily, whether or not you were able to express your feelings, I have known since the first moment I walked into the Montague mansion that you and I were meant to be together. It may sound corny, 'love at first sight', but it's true."

Lily laid her head on his shoulder and they stood silently for some time, listening to the gentle melody of the orchestra. It was only the two of them, in their own little world, holding on for dear life on to what they had both learned could so easily be torn apart.

Abby popped her head through the curtain, startling them both. "There you are," she said, stepping out onto the balcony with Jeremy right behind her. "I wondered where you'd gone."

"Sorry, honey," Lily apologized. She tried to step away from Mack, but he held her tight.

"Did you ask her yet?" Abigail asked in a stage whisper.

"Not yet, love. Do you think now is a good time?" He smiled and winked at the little girl.

Lily felt completely out of the loop. "How come everyone here seems to know what is going on except for me?" she complained, subtly curving her hand around Kevin's arm as he led them all back inside. "Does someone want to explain what is really happening here?"

Abby laughed and nudged an elbow into Jeremy's rib cage. "I will. We've been collaberatating—"

"Collaborating," Mack countered with a chuckle.

"Yeah. That word," Abby agreed happily.

"*Who,* precisely, are we talking about?"

"You and Kevin, of course," Abby said.

"I think she wants to know who has been collaborat-

ing against—for—her." He looked down at Lily with a
tender smile and put his hand over hers on his sleeve.
"That would be your mother, Abby, and me."

"My *mother?*" Lily said. "You mean to tell me my
mother has been working to get the two of us together?
Impossible!"

"I would have said that, too," Kevin said. "But you
wouldn't believe what your mom can do when she puts
her mind to it."

"Collaborating," Lily said shaking her head.

"What about the question?" Abby broke in.

"What question?" Lily asked.

"This one," Kevin said. He grinned and dropped to
one knee, right in the middle of the crowded room. People immediately stopped talking to see what this situation was all about.

Lily was mortified. For a moment. And then she realized all her dreams were coming true.

"Marry me," Kevin said, grasping one of her hands
in both of his.

Excited murmurs spread around the room.

"I'm on my knee here," Kevin reminded her.

"Mom, answer the question," Abby urged.

"But there's so much I don't know about you," she
protested, unable to relinquish fully her earlier doubts.

"Marry me," he said again, "and you'll have a lifetime to discover the man behind the mask."

Part of her wanted to run away, as far and as fast as

she could. She was terrified of marriage, frightened of losing Kevin to terrorists or any of the other criminals he encountered on a daily basis.

But in the end, her heart won out.

"Get up off your knees, Kevin. I want to marry you."

He gave a shout that echoed against the walls. Then he leaped to his feet and wrapped his arms around her, kissing her lips, her cheek, her forehead, her nose.

People were watching, applauding and cheering them on, and she didn't care.

She laughed. It was the first time in her life she had felt truly happy. Protected. Loved.

"You're lucky, Mom," Abby said, giving her a big hug. "You get to marry an angel."

Lily laughed. "Well, I don't know about that, but I do know I'm marrying the best, kindest, gentlest man in the whole world. And I've never been happier."

* * * * *

Dear Reader,

I don't have to ask you if you've ever been in a situation where you didn't feel in control. It's happened to the best of us.

As in Lily's life, as the cliché goes, bad things happen to good people. None of us is perfect, and we all make wrong decisions, which end up hurting other people and often ourselves.

Are you ripped apart inside because of what had been said or done? Do you wish you could go back and do things over, make all your wrongs right?

I know Lily did.

But, dear reader, I hope this book will remind you that control was never yours to begin with. It belongs to God! And God, my dear reader, you can always count on.

He truly is the strength of our lives—of whom, then should we be afraid?

I love to hear from my readers! You can write me at:
Deb Kastner
P.O. Box 481
Johnstown, CO 80534

Resting in His Strength,

Deb Kastner

Take 2 inspirational love stories FREE!

PLUS get a FREE surprise gift!

Mail to Steeple Hill Reader Service™

In U.S.
3010 Walden Ave.
P.O. Box 1867
Buffalo, NY 14240-1867

In Canada
P.O. Box 609
Fort Erie, Ontario
L2A 5X3

YES! Please send me 2 free Love Inspired® novels and my free surprise gift. After receiving them, if I don't wish to receive anymore, I can return the shipping statement marked cancel. If I don't cancel, I will receive 4 brand-new novels every month, before they're available in stores! Bill me at the low price of $4.24 each in the U.S. and $4.74 each in Canada, plus 25¢ shipping and handling and applicable sales tax, if any*. That's the complete price and a savings of over 10% off the cover prices—quite a bargain! I understand that accepting the books and gift places me under no obligation ever to buy any books. I can always return a shipment and cancel at any time. Even if I never buy another book from Steeple Hill, the 2 free books and the surprise gift are mine to keep forever.

113 IDN DZ9M
313 IDN DZ9N

Name	(PLEASE PRINT)	
Address	Apt. No.	
City	State/Prov.	Zip/Postal Code

Not valid to current Love Inspired® subscribers.

Want to try two free books from another series?
Call 1-800-873-8635 or visit www.morefreebooks.com.

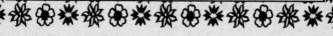